BETR

BETRAYAL 2

By

Denise Hill
Dwuna Henton
Penny Burt
Shatika Gray
Tammy Jackson

BETRAYAL 2

DH Books published by
DH Publishing Company
P.O. Box 333
Indianapolis, IN 46250

ISBN: 978-1-7336502-9-8
Book Cover Design: DH Publishing Company
www.DHpublishingco.com

Printed in the United States of America

DH Books

BETRAYAL 2

ACKNOWLEDGEMENT

Wow, what can I say book number ten for me. God, thank you for allowing me to continue to do what I love to do which is to bring my characters to life through my writing. I want to thank you for allowing me to work with such amazing women and writers. I want to thank my support system my son Daniel Powell and my daughter Devin Hill. I also want to thank my readers. Look out for the Betrayal pilot coming this fall to a theater near you! Denise Hill

I give honor to God who gives me beauty for ashes and connected me with my amazing co-authors on this fantastic project. I deeply appreciate my coauthors for accepting me on an already established team and helping me find my voice. I thank my parents for their encouragement and for being lifelong supporters of my writing. I am also eternally grateful for my two heartbeats, Jasmine and Janiyah, who keep me motivated and inspired every day. Last but not least, thank you, readers, for your investment and for joining us on this journey. Shatika Gray

First and foremost, I thank you, God! Thank you to my family and friends who continue to support and encourage me to not give up! I thank you my fellow Co-Authors for your hard work and dedication in creating another great novel. And to our readers, thank you so much for your support! Tammy Jackson

I thank God for the gift of writing and establishing this gift too shall make room for me. I thank Denise Hill for graciously being patient at times during this project when my life was being lived literally day by day. I appreciate the opportunity to collaborate with you and my co-authors/

sisters who also supported me during this project! Ms. B. you kept me on my toes and patiently waited for this novel to be completed two days after reading the first one! I thank my family and friends for supporting me, especially my husband and LA Tay Rari for encouraging and believing in the success of the Betrayal novels. To our readers, I hope you enjoy reading this one as much as you did the first.
Penny Burt

To all my real supporters (YOU AND I KNOW WHO YOU ARE). Thank you for always having my back, no matter what, and for believing in me so much! God puts people in your life for a reason, a season, or a lifetime. Your presence in my life has its definite reasons, and I know you will forever hold a special place within your hearts for me, as I will yours. Words fail to express my level of appreciation for you all. Your "nothing is impossible" attitude is out of this world and I thank the Lord daily for placing each of you in my life. Your prayers, unwavering faith, commitment, and support have been invaluable and all of you are unquestionably worthy of praise! You guys are the epitome of what true friends and family represent, and I am truly GRATEFUL! A simple thank you isn't enough. To the readers that we've gained from Betrayal I. I hope you enjoy Betrayal II as much and will be future readers and supporters.
Love, peace, and appreciation always.
Dwuna Henton

BETRAYAL 2

Prologue

Later that evening after Trina had left, Rodney prepared dinner for the two of them.

"You want the main course first or the dessert?"

"It all depends on what's for dessert?"

Rodney grabbed his dick.

"This is for dessert."

"I always like a little dessert before the main course," Candice said seductively.

Rodney lay on his back as Candice made her way down his body. She came to a stop when she reached his pipe.

"I forgot how big you were."

Rodney enjoyed the feeling of Candice's lips wrapped around him.

"Shit! That feels so damn good! You always knew how to work that mouth."

BETRAYAL 2

CHAPTER 1

That morning at work, Frank sat at his desk. He pulled out his phone and sent a text message to Thomas.

"Hey, what's up?" Thomas asked as he walked into Frank's cubicle.

"I have to do it. I have to tell HR what I know."

"Do you think that's wise?"

"If it were you, wouldn't you want someone to come forward and clear your name?"

"Yes, but why does it have to be you?" Thomas asked.

"Who else would it be?"

"How do you know you can trust Mr. Chris's old white ass?"

"I don't."

"Well, just be careful."

Frank exited the elevator and nervously looked around to see if anyone was in the hallway as he followed the sign towards H.R.

Frank walked up to the receptionist.

"Hi, I don't have an appointment, but I need to speak with Mr. Chris it's urgent. My name is Franklin Bonds."

"Mr. Chris doesn't usually see people without an appointment, but let me check with him. You can have a seat, and I'll let him know you're out here."

"Ok, thank you."

Frank sat down and waited in the lobby.

A few minutes later, the receptionist walked back out to the lobby where Frank was sitting.

"Mr. Bonds, you can go on in."

Inside the office, Mr. Chris stood. He extended his hand out to shake Frank's hand with a smile.

11

"Hello, Mr. Bonds. How may I help you?"

"I have some information that will help with the fraud investigation."

"Oh, really. Well, in that case, have a seat."

"Mr. Chris, you asked me yesterday about taking the lie detector test. I signed the form to take it, but now I can't take it."

"And why is that?"

Frank rocked back and forth in his chair. He was nervous. He didn't know if he could trust this man or not.

In the meantime, Karen and Susan stepped off the elevator and looked around the hall as they headed for Mr. Chris's office.

"I know he's in there. I overheard him and Thomas talking this morning."

"What's the problem, Frank. You can trust me."

Mr. Chris leaned forward and looked Frank in the eyes.

"Are you involved?"

"No, but I know who is."

Just then, they heard a knock at the door. Frank looked at the door and back at Mr. Chris.

"Sir, no one can know I am here!" Frank said nervously.

"You'll be okay."

Mr. Chris got up and opened the door.

"Well, well, what brings you ladies here? Come on in, Frank here was just about to tell me who's involved in the embezzlement."

Frank panicked. He saw the side door and looked back at Mr. Chris as he stood at the door with Susan and Karen. Frank got up quickly and eased out the side door that led to the conference room. When Mr. Chris turned around, the conference room door was cracked open, and Frank was gone. Susan and Karen walked inside. Karen saw that the

12

conference room door was cracked open. She walked over to the door and stuck her head inside, but there was no sign of Frank.

Thomas looked up to see Frank as he rushed back to his desk. Thomas rushed over.

"How did it go?" Thomas asked

"Those sneaky bitches showed up. I had to sneak out the side door."

"What! How did they know you were up there?"

"I have no idea, but if they want to be sneaky. I can be sneaky too. Frank pulled out his cell phone.

Stephanie was at home doing some homework when her phone rang.

"Hello."

"Good morning Stephanie, this is Frank. Do you have a few minutes to talk?"

"Yeah, what's going on?"

Frank began to tell Stephanie what happened.

"What! Aw hell naw! Let me get Detective Morris on the phone. I'll call you right back."

"Okay," Frank said.

Stephanie quickly dialed Detective Morris.

Detective Morris had just stepped out of the Men's room when his phone rang.

"Hello, this is Detective Morris, how can I help you?"

"Good morning, Detective Morris. This is Stephanie Taylor."

"Good morning Stephanie. Is everything okay?"

"No."

Stephanie began to explain.

"Well, it looks like I need to make another visit to

Charles Schwab this morning, but this time to see Mr.
Chris."

"Detective, I am worried about Frank. What if they try
to harm him?"

"Tell him to stay in a secure area where people can see
him until I get there. I'm heading out now."

"Thank you, detective."

Twenty minutes later, Frank sat at his desk. Susan and
Karen walked up.

"Frank, can we see you in my office."

"Nope, I don't think so. Whatever you two need to say
to me, you better say it right here."

Susan looked over at Karen.

Karen leaned over and whispered to Frank," Don't make
me drag yo ass!"

"Ha-ha! I wish the hell you would. You won't try and
drag anyone else.

Frank stood and planted his hands on his hips.

All heads turned when Mr. Chris stepped off the elevator
with Detective Morris and Detective Roy. Frank looked
over at Karen and Susan.

"Hey ladies, we would like to meet with you two in the
conference room."

"Sure," Susan said.

Susan and Karen looked over at Frank, who had a big smile
on his face.

Frank said softly, "Later bitches!" Frank popped his tongue
and rolled his neck.

Detective Roy spoke first, "I heard you two know
something about some wire transfers that were made to
look like Stephanie Taylor embezzled money from the
company?"

"I have no idea what you're talking about?" Susan said.

Mr. Chris chimed in, "Well, we can solve that. Tomorrow afternoon I want you two to take a polygraph test. That will prove everything."

"Sure, no problem," Karen said as her heart dropped to her stomach.

"You two are free to go. I will personally come and get you tomorrow."

Susan and Karen walked out.

"Let's take a ride down to the third floor."

Once they made it to the third floor. Karen scanned the area to make sure there was no one there.

"What the fuck is going on! We are going to jail!" Susan shouted.

"Calm down!"

"How the hell am I supposed to calm down. We have embezzled over a million dollars."

"You knew this could happen, so don't go acting brand new on me now!"

"Bitch! We were fine until you and that nutty professor decided to make another transfer, Susan said with her voice full of anger."

"You need to take responsibility for this too," Karen said.

"For all anyone knows, you came up with the plan, stole my information, and transferred money on your own," Susan said.

"Really, Is that how you want this to go down? You point the finger at Michael and me?" Karen asked.

"Damn right! I will throw you both under every bus in Indianapolis," Susan said.

"Well, at this point, it's your word against mine. Do whatever you got to do, bitch!" Karen said.

"I will... and all you need to do is take that polygraph

test and keep my name out of your mouth!"
Karen unfolded her arms, rolled her eyes, and walked toward the elevator in a rush.

Jason sat in his office staring at the walls when one of his employees stuck his head inside.

"Hey boss, are you okay!"
Jason looked up and smiled.

"Yeah, I am good. I'm just sitting here thinking."

"I see. Thinking about that babe you took to the cabins."

"How did you know about that?"

"I'm a good listener."

"You mean a good ear hustler."
Laughter filled the office.

"Well, all I know is that I heard enough to know something is going on between you two." Still partially laughing,

"Nothing's going on with us, she is a very good friend."

"Yeah, if you say so. She is a friend with benefits or one you wish you had benefits with."

"Okay, stop right there. I would never cross that line with her. She has been through a lot and I am there for her just as a friend."

"Hey, my bad. I'm just calling it as I see it."
The employee said as he put both hands up near his shoulders.

"Well, whatever you saw, you imagined it."

"Okay, okay... I just came in to say all the equipment is cleaned. I am about to head out."

"Thanks. I appreciate your hard work. Goodnight."

"You are welcome. Goodnight."
The employee closed the door as he exited.
Jason stared at the door. He shook his head and smiled. He

looked at Stephanie's picture on his phone and spoke to himself out loud.

Well, if we are just good friends, why am I constantly thinking about you? Why do I care what you think of me?"

CHAPTER 2

$\mathbf{T}$he next day, Ms. Wu opened the door to Mr. Chris's office and Susan followed her inside. The office looked like it had been transformed into an interrogation room. Ms. Wu motioned for Susan to sit at one end of the small table.

"Would you like some water?" Ms. Wu asked.
The sudden hospitality threw Susan off.

"Umm..., why? So you can steal my fingerprints and frame me for a crime I didn't commit? No, thank you!"
Susan gave Ms. Wu a nasty look as Ms. Wu hooked up Susan to the machine.

"Okay, then let's get started. I am going to ask you a few random questions to create a baseline."
Ms. Wu checked the paper in the machine and continued.

"Then, I will ask questions that are specific to the event."

"Don't you mean alleged event," Susan asked as she rolled her eyes? " I've watched plenty of crime shows. You aren't getting me."
Ms. Wu ignored Susan's attitude and remained professional.

"Please state your full name."
"Susan Marie Smith."
"State your date of birth."
"June 7, 1975."
"What city were you born in?"
"Indianapolis."
"When did you first discover the money transfers?"
"This is stupid!" Susan shouted.
"Please answer the question," Ms. Wu said.

Susan sighed, "I received a call from multiple clients reporting missing funds from their accounts."

"Was this the first time you knew about the missing funds?"

"Yes."

"Do you have access to all of the accounts in question?" Susan felt her blood pressure rise. She told herself to stay calm.

"Do you need me to repeat the question?"

"No, I mean, Yes. No, I don't need the question repeated. "Yes, I have access to all of the accounts.

"Did you transfer the money from the client's accounts?"

"No!"

"Did you conspire with someone to transfer money from the accounts?"

"No! That's it! I'm not answering any more of your questions."

Susan stood up and snatched off the connected wires. Ms. Wu remained calm.

"That's fine. We have all we need. Thank you for your cooperation. Follow me back to the conference room."

Susan felt like an idiot for her freak out. She trailed behind Ms. Wu into the conference room in silence.

Mr. Chris and Karen waited as Ms. Wu walked in and pulled Mr. Chris to the side. She quietly shared her results with him. After a few short minutes, Mr. Chris addressed Karen and Susan.

"Thank you both for participating in the polygraph. I know it wasn't easy for you."

Mr. Chris looked directly at Karen.

"That being said, Karen, you are free to go with my deepest apologies."

"Thank you, Mr. Chris! Thank you so much!"
Karen jumped up and dashed out of the room. Susan quickly stood in reaction. She was shocked.

"What! What about me?"

"Yes, what about you? That is exactly what I plan to discuss."

Mr. Chris looked Susan in the eyes. Susan had never seen this side of him before.

"You see, Karen and I had quite the chat and it appears that your polygraph test confirms what she told me."
Ms. Wu nodded in agreement.

"What are you talking about?"Susan asked loudly.

Mr. Chris raised his voice, "You know exactly what I am talking about! **YOU**, Ms. Smith, are the one we've been looking for all along!"

"I want my attorney!" Susan demanded.

"Call him... or her. We'll wait," Mr. Chris said sarcastically.

Two police officers walked into the conference room.

"Look... you have it all wrong. It wasn't me. It was Karen and her boyfriend, Michael. He kidnapped Judy."
Mr. Chris looked over at the two police officers and nodded his head.

The police officers walked over to Susan.

"Susan Smith, you have the right to remain silent. Anything you say....," The police officer grabbed Susan, stood her up, and placed her arms behind her back.

Tears began to roll down her face.

"Can and will be used against you in the court of law. You have the right to an attorney."

Susan jerked away from the officer and yelled.

"You have it all wrong!"

"If you cannot afford an attorney, one will be provided

for you," The officer continued.

Susan pleaded with Mr. Chris. "Please, don't do this!"

"Do you understand the rights I have just read you?" The officer asked.

"Fuck you!!!" Susan yelled out.

Susan tried to break free. The police gripped her tight as they walked her out of the conference room. Once the employees saw Susan escorted out in handcuffs. They stood as whispers filled the room.

Frank looked over at Thomas.

"What about that bitch ass Karen!"

JoJo sat inside his car on the phone.

"Nigga you better answer this fuckin phone. This is the fifth time I have called you."

Michael looked at his phone and let it go to voicemail.

"This mutherfucka better stop calling me. I will pay when I get good and ready."

"Hey, do you remember where his brother lives?" Tommy asked.

"Hell yeah!"

"Well, let's pay him a little visit. Maybe we can persuade his brother to tell us where he's hiding," Tommy said as he waved his gun.

JoJo and Tommy stood at the door. JoJo knocked twice before Gene opened the door.

"Can I help you guys?"

"Yeah, we're looking for Michael."

"Sorry, but Michael doesn't live here."

"Are you his brother?" Tommy asked.

"Yes, I am."

Tommy pulled out his gun and shoved his way inside.

"What the fuck!" Gene yelled as Tommy pushed him

21

backward. Gene tried to push back, but he was no match for Tommy.

"Where is Michael?"

Tommy pointed the gun at Gene.

"I told you he doesn't live here!"

"Okay, if he doesn't live here, where is he at?"

"I don't know! Michael doesn't tell me his whereabouts."

"What is the address to your mother's house? I'm gonna visit her to see if Michael's there!" JoJo asked.

"I'm not telling you that!"

JoJo placed the gun up to Gene's head.

"My beef ain't with you, it's yo lying brother, so put yo phone on speaker, call yo mom's, and get her to say the address."

"What am I supposed to say when she already knows I know the address?"

JoJo pushed the gun forcefully in Gene's jaw.

"Make up some shit!" Tommy said.

Gene pulled his phone out and dialed his mother's number.

"Hello."

"Hey, Ma."

"Boy, what do you want. I hope you didn't call to get me upset again?"

"Look, I just want to send you something nice to say I'm sorry for getting you upset the other day. I need to verify the address and zip."

"Awe how sweet of you, but you know this address has been the same since we moved here."

"Mom, I don't mean to cut you off, but I need to call the order in."

"It's 326 Marlette Drive, 6....."

Once they heard the address, Tommy pushed Gene to the

floor as they exited. JoJo dialed someone on his cell as they rushed out.

"Hey, Boss."

"What's up?"

"We on that fool Michael's trail."

"Good, and don't bring no extra heat my way, got it."

"Got it," JoJo said.

As soon as JoJo and Tommy left, Gene grabbed the phone and called Michael.

"Hey, they are headed your way. Get mom out of there!"

"What are you talking about?" Michael asked.

"Your thug friends just paid me a visit looking for you!"

"And you told them where I was!"

"I had no choice! It was either that or get my head blown off."

"Where are we going to go?"

"You can bring mom to me, but you can't stay here. You will not be satisfied until you get one of us killed behind your shit!"

Three hours later, Michael and his mom arrived at Gene's.

"I'm so glad we're here," Michael's mom said.

"Yeah, So am I."

Gene walked out and around to their mom's side of the car and opened the door.

"Hey, pretty lady, 1 am so glad to see you!" Gene said to his mom.

Gene kissed his mom on the cheek, and Michael came around to kiss her too.

"Mom, go on in, I will bring your bags in."

"Ok, and be safe Michael."

"I will ma."

Michael and Gene walked to the trunk to get their mom's bags.

"I got them and you can get the hell out of here!"

"Damn man, so that's how it is?

"Hell yeah! I just had my life threatened because of you, and you put our mother's well-being at risk."

"I'm sorry, man."

"Yeah, I hear you. Change yo ways man."

Michael's phone rang. He waved goodbye to Gene.

"Hello, babe, how's everything?"

"I'll start with the good news," Karen said.

"Lay it on me, I need some good news right about now."

"Susan and I had to take a lie detector test, and she didn't pass. I blamed everything on her, and the idiots believed me!"

"Really, so now what are they gonna do?"

"Susan was arrested. None of this would have even taken place if it hadn't been for that nosey ass Frank."

"Frank?"

"Yes, somehow he found out and was snitching all up and through H.R. You need to handle that."

"I'm on it."

CHAPTER 3

Jason's home morning

Jason rolled over to find Marsha staring up at the ceiling.

"How did you sleep?"

"Like a baby. I could get used to this."

"Well, don't."

Marsha looked over at Jason.

"Don't look at me like that."

"You know what. I don't get you. One minute you're hot, and the next minute you're cold as ice."

"You know how I am about having a female sleepover." Marsha said sarcastically, "Hmm. I bet if I were Stephanie, you wouldn't have a problem with it."

Marsha got up, grabbed her clothes, and headed for the bathroom. Jason continued to lay as he looked up at the ceiling. He said softly and smiled, "Yeah, you're right about that."

Later that afternoon, Jason sat on his couch thinking about Stephanie. He picked up his phone and dialed Stephanie's number, and it went to voicemail. Jason quickly hung up and started to focus his attention on the TV when he heard a knock on the door. When he opened the door, there stood Marsha.

"What are you doing here?" Jason said with irritation in his voice.

"Is that any way to greet a friend?"

Marsha pushed her way inside.

"I'm sorry. I'm just not in a good mood right now. I have a lot on my mind."

"What you need is to get out of this house."

"No! Marsha, did you hear what I said?"

"Shh. I have something planned so trust me this one time."

She pulled Jason close and ran her hands over his shoulders.

"You're so tense. I guarantee you what I have planned will be so relaxing."

"Relaxing, huh?"

"Very!"

"I was about to get something to eat," Jason said.

"I got that covered as well."

Jason shut the TV off, grabbed his keys, and they both headed out.

"Where are we going?"

"You will see," Marsha said as she pulled into the parking lot.

Ten minutes later, Jason and Marsha lay face down on the massage tables.

"You really surprised me with this massage. Thank you."

"I'm so glad you trusted me."

Marsha raised up and whispered to her masseuse. The masseuse motioned to her partner as they quietly exited the room.

Marsha stepped over to her purse next to the flower arrangement and pushed the record button on her phone. Marsha walked over to Jason and resumed where his masseuse left off. Her hands moved to his lower back, and her fingers touched his upper butt cheeks. Jason lifted his head quickly and turned to look.

26

"What! I should have known."

He shook his head and laughed.

Marsha went over to the table and brought back a strawberry and a scoop of whip cream. She put the fruit in his mouth and put the whipped cream on his nipples, licked it off, as her hand slipped under his towel.

Jason pulled Marsha's towel off and smeared whip cream on her nipples down to her belly button. He licked it as she moaned.

"Turn around and let me massage you down," Jason said.

"Ooooh!"

Jason turned her around and bent her over the massage table. He massaged her back, then he inserted himself inside her. Marsha glanced back in the direction of the camera from time to time.

"Stand up and turn around," Jason said.

Jason placed her legs over his shoulder. They looked into each other's eyes as they erupted into a quiet climax.

"This was just what I needed," Jason said as he planted kisses on her back.

"Yeah, me too!"

"You made reservations before checking with me?" Jason said as they made their way to her car.

"Yes, I didn't think you would mind a surprise," Marsha said as she winked at him.

"Thank you. I feel good."

"I know, it was fun for me, especially when I heard you yelp or whatever that sound was you made.

They laughed.

"Yeah, well, she applied pressure when I was not expecting it," Jason said as he grinned.

"I took a pic when you were not expecting it. You were

drooling laying over there."

Marsha showed Jason the picture.

"Hey, delete that!"

They struggled with the phone. Then Jason pulled her close to him, and they kissed in the parking lot.

"Um... You know I love dessert before dinner."

Jason laughed.

"Woman, get in the car."

Jason held the car door open for Marsha.

Stephanie closed her laptop and neatly assembled her books and papers next to it. She tilted her head back and spoke.

"Man, am I glad I finished that paper! I did not know school was this hard these days!"

She got up from her desk and grabbed her phone off the bed. She glanced at it, then put her hand on her stomach as it grumbled.

"All that hard work made me hungry!" She said as she stretched.

She unlocked her phone and looked up Fogo de Chao. She dialed the number and made a reservation for one.

She hopped in the shower and stood as the hot water hit her skin. She held her head back and let the water cover her face. She grabbed the soap and began to lather her entire body. Just then, a flashback of her and Jason popped into her head.

Stephanie pushed her way past Jason and stepped inside his home. She saw Marsha. Stephanie turned to Jason and apologized. She rushed past him and went out the front door. She ignored his attempt to explain.

Stephanie rinsed the soap from her face, opened her eyes, and frowned.

Why in the world is Jason on my mind? We are just good friends.

Stephanie got out of the shower and got dressed.

At Fogo de Chao, Stephanie stood in the lobby area and waited to be seated. She looked for a host or hostess and then began looking through her messages.

"Hello, ma'am! Do you have a reservation?" The hostess asked.

Stephanie jumped. "Oh! Yes, I have a 5 p.m. reservation."

The Hostess scrolled through the list on the tablet device.

"Is your name Stephanie?"

"Yes, that's me."

"Just one, right?"

"Yes, it is just me."

"Right this way, please."

The hostess seated Stephanie. She saw her green card on the table and left it. Stephanie scanned the seating area as she waited for the servers to come with hot skewers of meat.

"Hello. My name is Anna and I'm your server. Would you like something to drink? Soda or wine?"

"I'll have a bottle of San Pellegrino water and a glass of Moscato, please."

"Okay, I'll bring those right out."

Stephanie looked around the restaurant. Her eyes froze at the sight of Jason and Marsha.

Stephanie spoke quietly to herself.

"What the hell?"

Stephanie stared at the two as they smiled and talked. She saw them tussle over Marsha's phone, "I cannot believe this shit! I knew they were not..."

Stephanie held her words, closed her eyes, and took in a

deep breath to calm herself. She opened her eyes and looked in their direction again. *Why am I upset? Jason and I are only friends.*

As she stared, her mind flashed back to all the times she and Jason shared during her divorce ordeal.

At the cabin, Jason turned Stephanie's face towards him with his finger, and their eyes locked on each other. Jason bent down to hug Stephanie. Stephanie smelled the cologne Jason had on, and she looked up into Jason's eyes.

On her porch after they arrived back from the cabin, Jason asked her, "If you're not too tired of seeing this face, I was wondering if I could bring dinner back."

"I'm never too tired to see the warm face of a friend. A handsome friend at that."

Stephanie snapped out of her daze. She realized her thoughts were a deep desire for Jason.

"Oh shit!"

Stephanie quickly stood.

"I have got to get the hell out of here before he sees me."

Stephanie grabbed her purse and darted past the hostess and through the doors.

Jason and Marsha were in a deep conversation when he happened to see Stephanie dart out of the restaurant.

"Hold that thought, I'll be right back."

Jason jumped up and swiftly walked to the door.

"Stephanie! Stephanie," Jason yelled loudly.

Jason ran to her car. Stephanie turned and looked dead at Jason and gave him the middle finger.

"I can't believe him!" Stephanie said.

She wiped the tears with her hand. Stephanie continued to drive.

"He said he wasn't dating her! He's no better than

Desmond's ass!"

Jason walked back to the table.

"You are so disrespectful," Marsha said with an attitude. Marsha put her hand up to her face and looked directly at Jason.

"You're here with me having dinner, and then you see that bitch and forget all about me and run after her!"

"I apologize! I just didn't want her getting the wrong idea..."

Marsha cut him off.

"About us? Yeah, let's talk about us. What the fuck are we doing?"

"Marsha, let's not do this here," Jason said when he noticed some of the customers looking over at them.

Jason and Marsha finished their meal and went back to Jason's. As soon as they walked in, Marsha went at it.

"I don't understand you, Jason. Everything was so good between us until Stephanie. What is it about her?"

Marsha stood with arms folded across her chest as the tears fell.

Jason moved to stand in front of her.

"What do you want me to say? What do you want me to do? I've already apologized. I am so sorry that you feel I disrespected you."

"What is it going to take for you to see how much I love you?"

"Whoa! Whoa! You are moving a little too fast."

Jason shook his head.

"I like you, but I'm not trying to be in a relationship with you. I thought I made that clear."

Marsha grabbed her purse.

"You wouldn't know a good thing if it bit you in your fuckin ass!" Marsha stormed out.

31

CHAPTER 4

Stephanie sat on the couch with a bottle of Moscato white wine as the tears fell.

"Why am I crying? It's not like we are dating. I'm not even interested in..." She stopped to think.

"Am I attracted to Jason? Damn! That's why I have been feeling the way I have when it comes to him."

The next day, Stephanie sat at the kitchen table with her laptop when she heard a knock at the door.

When she opened the door, she was surprised to see Frank.

"Frank. What are you doing here?"

Frank looked at her sideways.

"Do I need a reason to visit?"

Stephanie shook her head.

"No silly, come on in."

"So, where were you yesterday? I stopped by to see if you wanted to go to dinner."

"I actually went out for dinner and ended up leaving before I got my food."

"Why?"

Stephanie waved her hand.

"Long story."

Frank's head bobbled.

"Honty, I got all day."

Stephanie laughed.

"You are so silly. I just overreacted when I saw Jason having dinner with another woman."

"And why would that bother you?

Frank looked directly at Stephanie.

"Aw... I see. Someone catching feelings for someone."

"No... no, it's not like that! I... I..."

32

Frank rolled his neck.

"I what!"

The doorbell rang.

Stephanie peeked through the keyhole and looked back at Frank.

"Damn!" Stephanie said as she backed away from the door. "Can you get the door for me? And tell him I'm not here."

Stephanie ran down the hallway.

Frank walked over to the door and opened it to find Jason standing there.

"Damn!" Frank said as he looked Jason up and down.

"Hi, Jason. How are you?"

"Hey Frank, where's Stephanie?"

Frank popped his tongue and waved his hand in the air.

"She's unavailable, but I'm free all day," Frank said seductively.

Jason gave Frank a crazy look as he moved past him.

"Stephanie, I know you're here so come on out, we need to talk!"

Stephanie moved slowly into view.

"I have nothing to say to you, Jason."

Jason stood in front of Stephanie.

"I would say you do. You gave me the middle finger, and for what? What did I do to deserve that?"

"I'm sorry, I don't know what came over me."

"Maybe it was her seeing you with another female that she didn't like."

Stephanie and Jason both turn to look at Frank as he stood with his arms crossed.

"Just saying. It's obvious that you two have some feelings for each other, but Steph if I'm wrong...," Frank popped his tongue.

"I will take him off your hands."

Frank walked over to Jason as he eyed him up and down.

"What big arms you have, and they match your thighs, I wonder what else they match?" Frank said as he looked Jason up and down.

"Frank," Stephanie yelled.

Jason laughed as he took Stephanie's hand.

"Stephanie, I really need to talk to you."

Jason looked over at Frank.

"In private." Jason looked back at Stephanie.

"Well, damn! I can take a hint," Frank said.

Jason looked back at Stephanie, "Is that alright?"

Stephanie had butterflies in her stomach. She stared at the floor, afraid to look up into Jason's eyes.

"Yes," Stephanie said shyly.

Stephanie turned to Frank.

"Frank, do you mind if we catch up some more tomorrow?"

"Oh! So it's like that? One word from tall, dark, and handsome, and I'm kicked to the curb!" Frank said jokingly.

"Whatever, Frank! You're so silly! You know it's not like that."

Stephanie walked Frank to the door. Frank pretended to be appalled.

"I thought it was hoes before bros! That coo' I didn't want to stay anyway. Girl, bye! Oh, and just make sure you're honest about your feelings with him." Frank whispered to Stephanie as he hugged her.

"Bye, Frank."

Frank winked at Stephanie as she playfully pushed him out the door.

Jason walked up behind Stephanie as she closed the door.

She turned around and saw the most beautiful man. Jason stood over her and took her hand again.

"Can we talk now? I really need to clear the air."
Stephanie bit her lip and looked at the floor.

"Ok, this sounds serious. Let's go into the living room."
Stephanie slid her hand out of Jason's and walked around him to the living room. Jason followed.
Stephanie and Jason sat on the couch facing each other.

"Steph, I really enjoy spending time with you."

"Me too, Jason. What's this about?"

"Last night, when I saw you run out of the restaurant, I realized something."

"You did? What did you realize?"
Stephanie fidgeted with her hands in her lap.

"I realized that I never want to be the one to cause you pain. I want to be the one that helps take the pain away."

"And how can you do that, Jason?"
She stood, Jason hesitated, "I want to be the man in your life that can show you love, compassion, loyalty, fun," Jason laughed, "and good sex."
Stephanie blushed, "What? But... what about Marsha? You know, I don't share."

"You won't ever have to. Marsha and I are just friends. There's nothing for you to worry about."

"Are you sure? Y'all looked pretty cozy together."

"Yeah, that's what Marsha would like you to think. I just need you to know that you're the only one I want."

"I'm not sure if I'm even ready, Jason. I want to. I just don't know how to move forward."

"I know you're still hurting, and that's ok. I'm not going anywhere. Whenever you're ready, I'll be here."
Jason walked over to Stephanie and gave her a long intimate hug. She took in the smell of his cologne and

35

melted in his arms. Stephanie whispered in his ear.

"You promise?" She said softly.

Jason pulled his head back and looked deep into Stephanie's eyes. He held her and moved her hair behind her ear.

"I promise."

Jason leaned in for a kiss and Stephanie met him halfway. After the kiss, Jason wiped a tear off of Stephanie's cheek. She kissed the palm of his hand.

"I'm going to hold you to that promise," Stephanie said.

"Yes, ma'am! I hope you do. Thanks for hearing me out."

Jason gave her a gentle peck on the forehead. Stephanie smiled sheepishly.

"Can we take it slow?"

Jason took Stephanie's hand in his and locked fingers.

"We'll take it as slow as you like."

"Thank you. I really don't want to rush into anything."

"I know. Don't worry about it. I got you, Steph. Speaking of which, it's getting late. I should probably go."

Jason got his keys and moved toward the front door. Stephanie followed.

The next day, Marcus rang the doorbell. He heard a noise on the other side of the door.

"Who is it?" Demetrius asked.

"My name is Marcus Slay. I was told I could find Demetrius Walker at this address. Is he here?"

Demetrius pulled back the curtain and looked out at Marcus.

"I'm Demetrius. What you want with me?"

"I just need to ask you some questions about Rodney Jackson."

"Look, I don't fuck with the cops, I have nothing to say about Rodney."

"I'm not a cop, I'm a private investigator working on behalf of Rodney."

Marcus took his badge off and showed it.

"I just need to get some information to help Rodney. It seems he has been wrongfully convicted of murder."

Demetrius opened the door and invited Marcus in. He motioned for Marcus to have a seat on the sofa. He then sat down next to Marcus.

"Thanks for inviting me in. As I said, I need any information you have that could help Rodney's case."

"What makes you think I know anything about Rodney's case?"

"Let me cut to the chase. I wouldn't be here if you didn't know anything about Rodney."

"All I can say is that Rodney and I ran in similar circles... and occasionally we came face to face."

"So you and Rodney are not close?"

"No, we were at one time, but that's dead."

"Why aren't you close anymore?"

"We did not see eye to eye about where and how we conducted business. But that was a long time ago."

"Business? I didn't know you did business with Rodney."

"Man come on... I didn't. We had to work out some differences to make sure each of our businesses made a profit."

"Yeah, I read about those profits you made. So who are the members of his circle?"

"I told you we ain't close like that! I don't know everybody he knows, besides the street talks."

37

"They do talk... but I'm not hearing anything to help Rodney's case. So, what can you tell me? Anything?"

"I can't tell you nothing, but there is this dude named Trey, who might be able to help."

"Trey... who?"

"Trey Jones. Rodney rarely went places without him. He may know something. You didn't hear his name from me though."

"I told you I am not a cop. I'm just trying to help Rodney's case. I don't disclose private info."

"Listen, man, whatever you do, understand I don't want no smoke. I got kids to raise and protect."

"Real talk. I appreciate you letting me in and name-dropping. Thank you. Hopefully, Trey will help me."

"You're welcome. Now, if you'll excuse me, I got someplace to go."

Demetrius led Marcus towards the door.

Natalie Cole played in the background as he prepared breakfast for his wife to be.

Desmond sang loudly, "I got love on my mind. I got love on my mind, and there's nothing particularly wrong."

Desmond held a broom in his hand, he acted as a performer on stage. He spun and slid over to the stove to finish breakfast.

"Good morning baby, Wow, you're in a great mood I see."

"I am in a great mood every day."

Desmond prepared a plate for Candice.

"I have the love of my life here with me and soon to be Mrs. Taylor."

Desmond planted a kiss on her forehead and placed her breakfast in front of her with a glass of orange juice.

38

Candice picked up the orange juice and sipped it. Desmond wrapped his arms around her and put his hands on her belly. He noticed that she had another wedding magazine.

"I can't wait until our baby is born! I'm going to spoil her so much," Desmond said.
Candice tried to ignore him and stuffed her mouth with food.

"I will give her everything. You know you have made me the happiest man, Candice!"

"I'm happy too. Why'd you give me so much food?"

"Because you're eating for two now!"
Candice was annoyed. She had no plans of blowing up. She had to keep her figure just the way Rodney liked it.

"Ok. Pass the syrup. Don't you have somewhere to be, babe?"
Desmond gave her the syrup and stood by the counter.

"Yeah, I better get going. I'm going to the gym, then I'm stopping by the barber shop for a haircut, and then I'm running by my mom and dad's house."
Candice mustered a smile. She was happy to hear that he'll be out of her hair all day.

"Ok, bye," Candice said.
She waved at him to rush him off.

"What are you doing today?" He asked as he turned around.

"Just working on some wedding stuff."
Candice picked up the wedding magazine and ruffled through it.

"Ok, I can take a hint!"
Desmond moved toward her and kissed her on the cheek.

"Let me know if you need anything and don't forget to

take your prenatal vitamins. I read that it is really important for the baby."

Desmond left the room and picked up his song where he left off. A few minutes later, Candice heard him leave out the garage door.

"Damn! I thought he'd never leave!"

She rolled her eyes and took her half-eaten plate to the sink, and put it down the garbage disposal. Then she opened a cabinet and reached to the back as she pulled out a small bottle of vodka.

"Hello, my little friend," She said as she opened the bottle and threw back a sip.

"Aww. This pregnancy charade may be harder than I thought."

CHAPTER 5

Desmond entered a crowded barbershop. Many of the regular customers greeted him. Desmond walked up to a gray-bearded barber.

"Hey, Des. I'll be with you in a sec!"

"Yeah man, that's cool."

Desmond sat down and took a glimpse at the game on TV. Customers around him, rooted and made bets. The barber finished the customer in his chair and brushed off the seat.

"I'm ready for ya. You want your usual?" His barber asked.

Desmond nodded and hopped in the chair. The barber draped the cape around him and brushed off his clippers.

"So, how's it goin with the new Mrs?"

The barber began to cut his hair.

"Aww, man. You know how it is. She's obsessed over this wedding. Every time I turn around, there's a new magazine!"

Desmond shook his head.

"I swear, she's gonna cost me a fortune, but It's all good though."

Desmond laughed. The barber stopped and looked at Desmond.

"What about Stephanie? You've been together a long time. How'd she take the news?"

"I haven't talked to Stephanie since the divorce. I don't know how to tell her. Not sure she even cares anymore."

The barber continued to cut Desmond's hair in silence as he spun the chair around. Desmond's back faced the entrance when Jason walked into the barbershop. They do not see each other. Desmond heard another barber shout.

"Heyyy! If it ain't the top Business Man of 2020!"

"What's up, man. Cut it out."

The barber laughed and nudged the customer in his chair. Desmond sat there as he ear hustled.

"I heard you won a weekend stay in a cabin down in Gatlinburg."

"Yeah, it was cool."

"I hope you took that fine honey, you had on your arm at the award ceremony. Woo, man, I'd hit that in e'ry room!"

The customers erupted in laughter. Desmond burned with fury. Desmond was out of the chair and in the customer's face in no time.

"Oh, you would huh? How about I break your fuckin nose!"

The customer stood toe to toe with Desmond.

"What's it to you? If you know like I know, you would back the fuck up off me!"

"You better watch your damn mouth!"

"Don't do it, Des. You've been coming here since you were a little boy. Don't disrespect my place like this. Chill!"

"Jason, get yo boy!"

"Boy! We ain't boys no more!" Desmond yelled.

"What do you mean y'all, not boys anymore."

Desmond and the men in the shop turned to look at Jason.

"I'm out and I'll hit you up later."

"Man, what's going on?" The second barber asked.

"Long story, I'll let Desmond have the honors."

They gave each other a hand dap and Jason exited out the barbershop door.

"So spill it!" The barber said.

"Ever since my ex-wife and I split up, Jason and she have been hanging out. She was his date the night he got that damn man of the year award and she probably went with him to the cabin."

"Damn! We can see why you're upset and hurt," His Barber said.

The other barber chimed in, "But you don't even know if he took yo ex and you poppin off?"

"Man, you were about to get a beat down for nothing," One of the customers said.

"I highly doubt that," Desmond said.

"Everything your ex-wife did for you and the miscarriages she went through, you left her for this woman you barely know," His barber said.

He stopped and made eye contact with Desmond. Desmond started to speak but didn't.

"Right, So why do you care who your ex hangs out with you don't want her?" His barber asked.

"Exactly why do you care?" The other barber said.

"We had some good years together. The point is I can't believe you think it's ok for Jason to be sniffing around my ex?"

"You're happily engaged with a baby on the way, right?"

His barber asked.

"Right," but that is beside the point. Jason was my best friend. How would you feel if Hank over there was running behind Cindy?"

"You're right. I see your point."

"I don't. I don't understand why you're mad at Jason? A lot of men would jump at the chance to be with your ex-wife," The other barber said.

43

"Whatever, there are certain codes you just don't cross." An older gentleman in the shop chimed in, "Youngman, you're not going to like this, but you want someone to behave morally right by you when you weren't?"

"He's got a point man," His barber said.

"I can't believe this. Are you done?" Desmond asked.

"No, sir."

"I don't want to talk about it anymore. Did y'all see the game Sunday?" Desmond said as he quickly changed the subject.

Candice lay passed out on the couch. Her phone rang several times. She finally came to and answered. Candice said raspily, "Hello."

"Hello, may I speak to Candice Spencer?"

"Who's th-is?"

Candice slurred and rubbed her eyes.

"This is Vivian's Bridal. Your dress is back from alterations. I want to confirm your final fitting today at 2 pm."

"Oh, shit! Candice sighed. "What time is it?"

"It's 1:50 pm, ma'am."

"Ok... I'll be there."

"Thank you and you will need..."

Candice hung up, held her head, and groaned. She turned her head and the small bottle of vodka stared back at her from the coffee table.

"Ugh....," Candice sighed and rolled off the couch. She grabbed the bottle and headed upstairs.

The next day, Mr. Chris stepped off the elevator and walked over to Frank's desk. "Excuse me, Frank, can I see you in conference room three."

"Sure." Frank looked over at Thomas as he followed Mr. Chris into the conference room.

44

Inside the conference room, Frank sat around the conference table twiddling his fingers when he heard a knock at the door.

Mr. Chris got up and opened the door to find Detective Morris.

"Come on in, I was just about to have a conversation with Frank."

The detective took a seat.

"Frank, I want to thank you for your help."

"Yes, we couldn't have done this without you," Detective Morris said.

Frank looked at them with a puzzled look.

"So why wasn't Karen arrested?"

Karen wasn't involved. She passed her polygraph test.

Frank stood.

"That's bullshit, and you both know it. Karen and Michael were the masterminds behind this." Frank blurted out.

Frank looked over at the detective."

"I don't even feel safe here anymore, especially while Bonnie and Clyde are running around here free. Hell, I could be next on their list."

Detective Morris looked at Mr. Chris.

"He needs to know," Detective Morris said.

Mr. Chris nodded his head.

"Listen, you have to promise me you will not say anything to anyone. Can I trust you?"

"Of course," Frank said.

"I didn't arrest Karen, because I want her to lead us to Michael, but trust me, she will be arrested at some point."

"But until then, what about me? I don't feel safe."

"I can put you in witness protection."

"For how long?"

45

"For as long as I need to."

"Okay, but I need to take care of some things first. Can I go and do that now?"

"Yes, and when you are ready, meet me at the precinct," Detective Morris said as he handed Frank a business card.

Frank grabbed his belongings from his desk. He looked over at Thomas and whispered.

"I'll be in touch."

Thomas looked confused.

Frank stepped off the elevator on the 5th floor of the parking garage. As he got off the elevator, he looked around. He felt uneasy as he walked swiftly to his car.

Frank exhaled a sigh of relief and wiped his forehead once he was inside. He pulled out his phone and checked his messages.

A figure dressed in black emerged from the back seat and quickly put a rope around Frank's neck. He struggled to get his hand up under the rope, but eventually gave in. The assailant exited the back seat and ran off. Frank waited a few seconds, before exhaling as he struggled to catch his breath.

He continued to breathe as he reached for his phone and the business card that lay on the passenger seat.

Frank coughed continuously. He dialed the number on Detective Morris' business card and put the phone to his ear. He listened to the voicemail.

"Shit, Shit, Shit! What do I do now?"

Frank checked to see if anyone was around.

"I've got to get out of here. Maybe Mr. Chris can help me find Detective Morris," Frank said.

Frank grabbed his stuff, slowly opened his driver's door, and slid out of the car. He crouched down beside it. He softly closed the door. Bravely, Frank dashed to the elevator. He pushed the button.

"C'mon! C'mon, dammit!"

Frank's heart pounded intensely as he waited for the elevator to arrive. Every sound triggered his paranoia. The door opened, and Frank ran inside. He frantically pushed for the door to close.

The door closed, and Frank held his throat as he leaned back up against the elevator wall. The elevator opened, and there stood Karen. She tried unsuccessfully to hide her shock and disappointment.

Frank exited the elevator and quickly walked past Karen.

"Frank? What's wrong?"

He looked back at Karen.

"As if you don't know, Bitch!"

Frank walked down the hall to the conference room. Karen watched, stunned, and then moved swiftly to her office.

Frank burst into the conference room. Mr. Chris and Detective Morris turned their heads in astonishment.

"It was Michael... he tried to kill me!"

Mr. Chris and Detective Morris rushed to Frank's side.

In the shower, Desmond tried to wash off all the frustration from the day. He replayed the words from the barbershop. He could still hear the customer's laugh.

"Uggh! Why can't I let this go! Stephanie isn't even mine anymore. I shouldn't care who she fucks?"

Desmond grabbed a towel and got out of the shower.

"Who am I kidding? I'm always going to care."

Desmond slightly dried off. He heard Candice enter the condo and walk up the stairs.

Desmond met Candice at the top of the stairway with only a towel around his waist. Little beads of water glistened on his chest.

"Well, hello," Candice said. Candice smiled.

47

Desmond grabbed Candice and kissed her.

She dropped her purse beside her and wrapped her arms around Desmond. He dropped his towel and moved her hand to his erection.

"You like that?"

"Mm-hmm!"

He lifted her as she wrapped her legs around him. Desmond balanced her against the adjacent wall. He moved his hand up her skirt and put his fingers inside to test her wetness.

"Oh, you ready for me! I'm about to give it to you."

Candice moaned as Desmond inserted himself. He pressed her back against the wall while she moaned again. Candice pulled off her shirt and bra as Desmond sucked her nipples. Candice clawed his back with pleasure.

Candice whispered, "Let's go into the bedroom."

Candice nibbled on Desmond's ear and rubbed his head as he carried her. He kicked something on the way into the room. Candice noticed her vodka bottle, rolled to a stop by the bed.

"What was that?"

Desmond looked around.

"I'm sure it was nothing!"

Candice pulled him into another embrace as he lay her down on the bed. She pulled off her skirt and dropped it over the bottle.

"Turn over," Desmond said.

His tone gave Candice chills. Desmond stood on the side of the bed, and Candice turned over on her knees with hands in front. He stroked her from behind long and hard. She grabbed the sheets. He pulled her hair.

"Oh, Des!" Candice screamed.

Candice's breast flapped as his stroke intensified. They climaxed. Desmond collapsed onto her back, and soon they fell asleep.

CHAPTER 6

In lockup, Susan walked into the holding area as three middle-aged black women stopped in the middle of their conversation and glanced at her.

Susan took a seat on the wooden bench across from them.

"What you in here for baby doll?" The first black inmate asked.

Susan looked down and didn't answer.

"Oh, this bitch thinks she's too good to answer." The second black inmate said.

The third black inmate said, "In here bitch we all the same."

Susan continued to ignore the women as the tears rolled down her face. A white inmate noticed and slid over to her.

"Don't pay them any mind, but you will have to stand up for yourself or you will be a target," The white inmate said.

Susan raised her head and looked at the white inmate as she wiped the tears away.

"I don't belong here," Susan said.

"She says she doesn't belong here," The first black inmate said as the other inmates laughed.

"Neither do we," Another inmate said.

"Do you have a bond?" The white inmate asked.

"Yes. I called my mom and she and my brother will handle everything."

"That's good. This ain't no place for someone like you. In here, you can't trust anyone," The white inmate whispered.

"That doesn't sound much different than the corporate world," Susan said as she thought about Karen."

Karen paced back and forth as she talked over the phone. She was furious."

"I thought you handled the situation!" Karen yelled.

"I did."

"Like hell you did! Why did I just run into Frank about three minutes ago?"

"What!"

"Yes, that mutherfucka is still breathing. Do I need to handle this?"

"If you think you can do better, then handle the little nigga!" Michael said.

Michael disconnected the call.

Karen looked at her phone.

"No he didn't just hang up on me!"

Susan's Mom and her brother sat at the kitchen table.

"Thanks for coming over baby. Did you get the money together to pay Susie's bail?"

Susan's Mom stirred her coffee and took a sip.

"Mama, I was thinking about it and I don't think we should pay it."

Susan's Mom puts her mug down.

"Whatchu mean? I have some money in savings."

"I know, mama, but listen. The clerk says Susan's bond is $100,000. That means we would have to pay $10,000."

"$10,000! My Lord, where am I supposed to get that much money! Maybe, I could get a second mortgage on the house."

"Absolutely not! You cannot afford another mortgage. You're barely making it by as it is," Her son said with a stern voice.

"Susie can pay me back."

"No, she won't! When has she ever paid you back for money that she has borrowed from you?"

"What are we going to do?"

"Nothing! She made her bed, so let her lay in it. We need to make her pay for her actions like we didn't do when she was younger."

"You mean to leave her in there? We can't! That's my baby girl!"

"Believe me, I know, mom. I don't want to either, but it's past time that she learns her lesson."

Susan's brother cupped Susan's mom's hand in his.

"Besides, you bailed her out enough when she was in juvie."

"But, your father..."

"Dad would agree with me. He wouldn't want you struggling."

Susan's Mom stood and walked over to an old family portrait.

"No, he wouldn't."

Susan's Mom hung her head. Susan's Brother stood behind her and put both hands on her shoulders.

"That child was always up to something. I just thought she had finally got some sense."

"Apparently not. The only reason she was able to get this job is because those records were sealed."

"You really believe she did it, don't you?"

"Mom, I've known Susie all her life. I'm almost certain she did everything they said she did."

Susan's Mom wept as her son held her close.

"I just can't believe it."

Susan cried and paced the cell. She grabbed the bars and yelled at the guard.

"I don't belong here! I don't belong here!"

"Quiet, Inmate!" The guard yelled.

The white Inmate urged Susan to come away from the bars.

Susan resumed to pace and talk to herself out loud.

"How did this happen? I can't believe I'm in here. I have to get out of here or I'll go crazy!"

"Relax. You said your mom and brother are on it. Besides, the courts are closed anyway. Better get comfy," The white inmate said.

"I can't. I need to get to Karen!" Susan said.

"Who's Karen?"

Susan stopped and stood against the wall. She looked at the white Inmate.

"She's the snitch that double-crossed me and got me thrown in here! But once I make bail, I'm gonna find her ass!"

"You know what they say about snitches," The black inmate said,

"Yeah... snitches get stitches," The second black inmate said.

"Exactly," Susan said.

Susan wiped her face and huddled with the three inmates as they moved closer to hear what happened.

"I can't wait to beat her ass, but I have to think of a way where she'll never see me comin'," Susan lowered her voice.

"Haha, I like how you think. You're gonna fit in just fine here," The 1st black inmate said boisterously.

The two black inmates walked over to another side of the cell. Susan and the white Inmate sat down.

"I thought you said you don't belong here."

"I don't, but that doesn't mean I won't fight back. If I go down, that bitch will be right beside me," Susan said.

"What are you gonna do?"

"Like I'd tell you! I don't know you like that. Trust no one, remember. I've already made that mistake once."

Candice heard her phone buzz loudly.

"What is that?" Desmond asked.

"It's my phone. I'll get it. Go back to sleep."

Desmond turned over. Candice recalled leaving her purse in the hallway. She slid out of bed and kicked something cold. Candice looked down.

"Oh, shit!"

Candice saw her empty vodka bottle spinning across the floor into the open. Desmond sat up in bed.

"What's wrong? Is it the baby?" Desmond asked.

"No, nothing! The baby is fine. I just, uh, hit my foot, I'm ok. You stay in bed," Candice said nervously.

Desmond laid down again. Candice grabbed her skirt from the floor, wrapped it around the bottle, and rushed toward her purse.

The floor creaked. Candice paused, she looked over at Desmond. He lay with his eyes closed. She finally reached the stairway.

How could I be so stupid! I almost got caught. No more drinking, Candice!

She shoved the bottle deep inside her purse when her phone buzzed again. She answered it.

"Hello."

No response. Candice looked at her phone screen and saw five missed calls and three voice messages. She went to her voicemail and pressed play.

The first message, "Where my sweet Candy at? You know I need my sweet Candy...," Rodney said.

Candice stopped the voicemail and went to the second message.

"Where you at? Why you ain't answering yo phone! You know I don't like it when you ain't answering yo phone!" This time Rodney was pissed.

Candice hesitated and then selected the third voice message.

By now Rodney is irate. "You need to come to see me now!! I borrowed my buddy's phone to call you and you over there laying around fuckin' that..,"

Candice deleted the voicemails. She felt torn.

What am I doing? Desmond is a good dude, but I love Rodney. Keep your head in the game, Candice.

Candice quietly gathered up her other clothes and put them on. She snatched her purse and headed downstairs. She intended to go to see Rodney.

Desmond appeared at the top of the stairs.

"Where are you going?'

Startled, Candice stopped on the stairs and turned around. She must think fast.

"Oh, The bridal shop called. They need me to come back for another fitting. I'll be back as soon as I can."

Candice rushed down the stairs before Desmond could object.

Later that evening, Marsha turned onto Jason's street just in time to see Jason pull off. She looked over at the food in the passenger seat.

"He's probably going to see that bitch."

She followed him at a distance and watch as he pulled into Stephanie's driveway. Stephanie met him outside. They got into his car and took off.

Marsha continued to follow them at a distance.

She followed them to the downtown canal. She quickly pulled into a parking spot and ran across the street.

She watched them get on the paddle boat ride.

"This is such a relaxing ride, and I loved it more having you to share it with," Stephanie said.

"I'm glad we talked without Frank."

Stephanie laughed.

"He meant well. It was good to lay out how we felt. I should have been more upfront," Stephanie said.

"We got our feelings all out in the open that's a good start. Well, it looks like we're at the end of our ride young lady."

Marsha watched as Jason stepped out and helped Stephanie out of the paddleboat.

"I'm going to go over to the ice cream vendor and get us some ice cream. You can go grab us a bench."

As Jason made his way over to the ice cream vendor, he heard his phone ring. He looked and saw it was Marsha and disconnected the call.

Marsha stood out of sight and saw Jason as he disconnected her call.

"Oh wow, really?" Marsha said.

Marsha dialed Jason's phone again.

Jason paid for his purchase when his phone vibrated in his pocket and he ignored it.

"I'm not the one, Jason. You just don't know, but I can play games too," Marsha said.

Marsha sent another message.

Stephanie sat on a bench and reviewed her messages while she waited for Jason.

Stephanie received a video from someone. She opened the video. She sees Jason and Marsha in a room having sex.

"What the..."

CHAPTER 7

Jason walked back over to Stephanie and saw the expression on her face.

"Steph, what's wrong."

Jason handed her the ice cream cone.

Stephanie shook her head and snatched the ice cream cone.

"What the fuck is this!"

"What is what?"

Stephanie showed Jason the video.

"This doesn't seem like someone not into someone look, just take me home," Stephanie said as she stood.

Jason shook his head.

"Look, can I explain something to you first?"

"Jason, right now, I don't want to hear shit from you. Just take me home, or do I need to call an Uber?"

"So you don't care to hear what I have to say?"

Stephanie gave Jason an evil look.

Marsha stood with a grin on her face as Jason and Stephanie argued.

Thirty minutes later, Jason pulled into the driveway. He put his car in park and cut the ignition. He turned to face Stephanie.

"Stephanie. You don't have to say anything, but just let me explain, okay?"

Stephanie nodded her head.

"Marsha and I are not a couple, we've never been a couple. It has always been just sex with us."

Stephanie turned to face Jason.

"Would Marsha agree that it is just sex with you two?"

"No, because she wants more and I don't. I want you and only you!"

"I don't know Jason. I don't have time for games, and right now, you seem to be playing games."

"How am I playing games?"

"You're playing with a woman's emotions, and that's not going to end well. You need to stop all communications with her before someone gets hurt!"

Jason ran his hand across his face.

"I guess you're right because I'm not trying to hurt anyone."

Marsha pulled onto Stephanie's street and parked about half-block down from Stephanie's home.

"What is he still doing there?"

Marsha grabbed the steering wheel.

"What is there to talk about! Jason, I know you just didn't fuck me, and now you're begging and pleading with that bitch!" Marsha said angrily.

"Marsha sent that video so she must think you changed your mind about her."

"No, she is manipulative and set that up. I'm telling you, think about it. I feel set up. That intimate moment she recorded without my knowledge wasn't cool, and then she shared it with you, to make you think more is going on with us than it is."

"I see your point, but that video she sent sure hurt. I can't get a break," Stephanie said.

Jason took his finger and gently placed it under Stephanie's chin. He turned her face towards him and looked into her eyes.

"Marsha and I have been sex buddies for a while now. When you and Desmond split up, I became attracted and wanted to be with you, but I didn't know how you felt about me so you can't hold that against me. I'm not playing games and there will be no more back and forth with Marsha, it's over."

Jason leaned in and kissed Stephanie on the forehead.

"Ok, please forgive me, but remember that encounter with her was before we poured our hearts out to each other. Can we start over?"

"Ok, clean slate Mr. Santiago."

Jason quickly got out of the car. He smiled and rushed to open Stephanie's car door.

"I can't believe this, you stupid bitch! I know you are not listening to him? Jason you one pleading mutha.."

Marsha watched as Stephanie stepped out of the car, and Jason gave her a long passionate kiss.

"What! You got to be kidding me! This didn't just happen."

Marsha drove off, she was pissed.

JoJo and Tommy arrived at Michael's mom's house.

JoJo approached the front door as Tommy walked around to the back of the house.

JoJo and Tommy burst in. They searched each room and met in the middle of the home.

"No sign of him," Tommy said.

"No sign of any of his stuff back there either, but the old woman's stuff look like she left in a hurry," JoJo said.

"Yeah, and the coffee pot is still on."

"We closing in on dat ass," JoJo said.

"Yeah, where to now?"

"To Indy to his girlfriend's crib. Some chick name Karen," JoJo said.

JoJo pulled out his phone and made a call.

"Yo, Blue, do you remember where Michael and his girl Karen stay?"

"Yeah... why?" Blue asked.

"I need you to put some eyes on the place and send me the address we headed there now."

"Ok, if we see him or his girl, what do you want done, should we snatch their ass or what?"

"No, just keep eyes on them. I'm gonna do the snatching."

"Bet."

JoJo and Tommy exited out the back.

Stephanie and Jason were asleep on the couch, fully clothed. Two empty wine glasses were on the coffee table next to an empty bottle of Moscato. Jason awakened and saw Stephanie as she lay on his chest. He moved the hair away from her face. Stephanie's eyes opened, and she looked at him.

"Jason?"

"Yes, I'm here."

"Oh my God. I thought it was all a dream, but you really are here with me."

Jason chuckled. "There's no place I'd rather be, Steph."

Jason hugged her. Stephanie smiled and sat up on the couch.

"Wow. What time is it? I can't believe we fell asleep watching that movie. I must look a mess!"

Stephanie attempted to fix her hair.

"You look beautiful as ever," Jason said as he looked at her.

Jason leaned in for a kiss. Stephanie gave in and put her arms around Jason's neck. Jason pulled Stephanie close as the kiss intensified. They lay back down on the couch, and Stephanie got on top. They fondled each other and kissed.

"I want you so bad right now."

Stephanie breathed heavily, "Me too, Jason."

They continued to make out. Jason reached up the back of

59

Stephanie's shirt to unfasten her bra strap, but suddenly stopped and pulled away.

"I'm sorry, Steph."

Stephanie sat up and adjusted her shirt.

"Sorry for what?"

"You said you wanted to take it slow, and here I am all over you."

"It's ok, you're not making me do anything I don't want to do."

"I understand, but you trusted me enough to invite me in last night, even after that stunt Marsha pulled."

Jason stood.

"I want to give you everything you need, and that starts with me setting things straight with Marsha. I should go."

Stephanie stood.

"Ok, I get that, but I don't understand why you have to leave?"

"Because Babe, if I stay, the way I'm feeling, we'd have to buy you a whole new couch after I'm done with you because I would be all up in your walls like I paint."

Stephanie giggled.

"Now that, I gotta see."

Jason grabbed Stephanie and gave her a long kiss.

"Ok, now I really gotta go."

"Ok."

Stephanie watched as Jason exited her home.

There was a knock on the door. Michael peered through the peephole and hesitated, then opened the door.

"What are you doing here, Karen?"

Karen walked past Michael and went inside. Michael looked around outside and then quickly closed the door. Karen walked over to the bed and sat down.

"I had to come to see you, Michael, since you wanna be

hanging up on people and shit!"
Michael sighed.

"Are you for real? What do you expect me to do? I thought he was dead!"
Michael stood in front of Karen.

"I expected you to handle the problem! Why do I have to do everything myself?"

"Oh, yeah? Everything?"
Michael pushed Karen down on her back and climbed halfway on top of her. Michael grabbed Karen's breast as they kissed heavily.

JoJo's men drove slowly through the motel parking lot in a utility van. Blue and Big Tony looked around.

"Hey Big Tony, are you sure this is where she went?"

"Yeah, she left the house and drove this way. See Blue! I told you. There's that bitch's car over there."

"Aight, coo'. I'mma call JoJo, and then we gonna figure out which room they are in," Blue said.
Big Tony parked the van. Blue took out his phone.

"Yeah."

"We got 'em, Jo," Big Tony said.

"Coo'. We just got back. Text me the deets. We're on our way."
Blue hung up, took his gun out, and checked the magazine. Blue smiled and inserted the magazine into place. Blue looked at Big Tony.

"We bout to have some fun."
Karen stopped and pushed Michael off.

"I'm serious, Michael! With Frank still running his mouth. If he testifies, we could go to prison for a long time. And I' ain't trying to do that."

"I promise, I will handle the little nigga."

"How? You couldn't handle it the first time," Karen said.

"Look, I said I got this. Now can we get back to this dick! I know you miss it."

Karen softens, "You're right."

Michael took off his shirt. Karen laid backward on the bed and pulled Michael down on top of her. They kissed and Michael lifted Karen's blouse.

He kissed Karen's belly and continued to plant kisses downward.

"I bet you missed this tongue too. I know what you need."

Karen nodded. Michael pulled off her skirt and panties. Karen puts her legs on Michael's shoulders as his tongue went deep inside her.

"Oh yes...," Karen grunted.

Karen continued to enjoy the tongue action, and then she started to panic.

"Shit! Stop. We can't do this. Get off me!"

Michael moved back. Karen sat up.

"Karen, Dammit. What is it now?" Michael said, annoyed at this point.

"I just have a bad feeling."

Karen got up and put her clothes back on.

"You and your fuckin' intuitions."

CHAPTER 8

Officer Lewis was in his late twenties. He was tall, dark, lean, attractive, and ripped. He heard Detective Morris on the walkie-talkie in the passenger's seat.

"I need an update on the subject's whereabouts."

Officer Lewis picked up his walkie-talkie and responded.

"Detective Morris, this is Officer Lewis. I have eyes on the subject's vehicle."

"Is she still at the office?" Detective Morris asked.

"Negative. She went home and then lead us right where we hoped she would."

"Good. Stay there! Send me your location, and don't let her leave. I'm on my way."

Big Tony checked his gun and tucked it under his shirt.

"Ok, so what's the plan, Blue?" Big Tony asked.

"You just follow my lead," Blue said.

Blue and Big Tony got out of the van as JoJo and Tommy pulled up beside them. They all were headed toward the office.

Michael got up and peeked through the blinds.

"Oh, Shit! I gotta get the fuck out of here NOW!"

"Why, what's wrong Michael? Who is it?"

"Fuckin' JoJo and Tommy. Damn. How did they find me? They're walking towards the office. Let's go!"

Karen grabbed her purse and opened the door. Karen and Michael exited the hotel room.

Officer Lewis sat up when he saw the door open. He picked up his walkie-talkie and informed Detective Morris of Karen's movement.

Karen had just exited the room with a male, possibly her boyfriend, Michael.

"10-4 Don't let her get away. I am a minute from the scene," Detective Lewis said.

"10-4," Officer Lewis replied.

Officer Lewis jumped from his car and ran towards Karen and Michael as they approached her car. Karen pulled her keys from her purse to unlock the door. Michael saw the officer coming and took off running.

Karen looked up and saw Michael as he started to run. She saw Officer Lewis as he approached and tried to hurry inside the car.

Officer Lewis stopped her before she could close the door.

"Drop the keys, Karen! Put your hands on the steering wheel where I can see them. 10-26, I repeat 10-26," Officer Lewis said.

Officer Lewis placed the cuffs on her hands and announced over the radio.

"10-95, I repeat 10-95... one suspect is in custody. The boyfriend fled on foot into the wooded area on the side of the motel."

Ahmad watched TV with his feet up and his back to the door. JoJo, Tommy, Blue, and Big Tony walked in. The bell rang on the door as they enter. Ahmad didn't turn around or look up.

Ahmad was in his middle forties a middle eastern heavy-set male.

"We're full," Ahmad said.

Ahmad continued to watch TV.

"Well, we're only lookin' fo' one room,' JoJo said.

"I said, we're...," Ahmad looked up in the mirror above the counter and saw the group of men behind him. Ahmad put his feet down and turned around. JoJo reached over the counter and grabbed Ahmad by the collar.

"You said, what, muthafucker?"

"I'm sorry, I'm sure there is at least one room I can find suitable for you."

JoJo released Ahmad. Tommy, Blue, and Big Tony looked around the office to make sure it's empty. Ahmad went to his computer.

"What's yo name," JoJo asked

"Ahmad."

JoJo sat on the counter and looked at the computer monitor.

"Ok, Ahmaaad. My name is JoJo. I'm lookin' fo' a friend, and you gonna tell me what room he is in."

"I... I can't give out that information."

"Oh, you can't? What about now, foo'?"

JoJo drew his gun and put it to Ahmad's head. Ahmad closed his eyes. Tommy, Blue, and Big Tony surrounded them.

"What about now, huh? I can't hear you, Ahmad? You wanna live?"

Ahmad noticeably glanced over at a picture of his kids under the counter.

'Yes! I wanna live."

JoJo grabbed the picture and threw it across the room. It broke against the wall.

"Give me da room number for Michael Jamison!"

Ahmad frantically typed on the keyboard.

"Room 174."

"Now, that wasn't so hard," JoJo asked.

JoJo put down his gun and got off the counter. Ahmad breathed a sigh of relief as JoJo backed away. JoJo leaned over to Blue.

"No witnesses," JoJo said.

Blue nodded. JoJo signaled to Tommy and they went out

the door. Big Tony stood watch by the door for Blue. Blue snapped Ahmad's neck and hid his body under the counter. Blue took down the security camera. Blue and Big Tony left.

Karen resisted as Officer Lewis pulled her out of her seat and to the side of the car.

"Let me go! I haven't done anything wrong. What the fuck! Why are you holding me?" Karen asked.

"10-4, I'm on the scene. Backup should be arriving soon," Detective Morris said.

Detective Morris pulled up, got out of his car, with a toothpick in his mouth, and approached Karen's car.

"What the hell is going on? Why am I being detained?"

"Come on Karen, I know you're smarter than that. We have been following your every move since we let you go," Detective Morris said.

"This is some bullshit. If I was free to go, why in hell am I being followed?"

"Karen, you didn't think we really believed you, did you?"

Karen stared at Detective Morris.

"We knew you would lead us to Michael, after all, he is an accomplice to the crime. Yet somehow he got away again," Detective Morris said.

"Good for him, y'all ain't nothing but some snakes anyway," Karen said.

"Well, on that note, Karen you are under arrest for embezzlement! You have the right to remain silent."

Detective Morris continued to read Karen her Miranda Rights as he placed her in the back of his car.

JoJo and his men stepped outside and saw the police as they put Karen in the back of the squad car.

They noticed two other officers as they ran toward the

woods on the side of the motel. They walked back to their car and sat inside and watched.

The officers searched for Michael.

"Let's split up," The first officer said.

The first officer went right while the other officer went left The trail led them right back to where they started.

"What the fuck! Where can he be?"

The officers walked out of the woods and back to the car.

"Don't tell me he got away," Detective Morris said.

The officers looked at Detective Morris. He threw his hands up in the air. "You two fucks couldn't catch a dog with no legs."

Michael sat up in the tree as he watched the officer take off with Karen in the back of the police car. He waited until they were out of sight before he climbed down. Michael walked back over to the motel. He slipped back in and looked for a place to hide. Michael heard someone coming. He forced the adjoining door open and hid in the next room.

JoJo and his men kicked down the door. They came in with guns drawn and looked for him.

"I know I saw Michael sneaked back in here. Turn over everything! If he's here, I'm gonna fuck him up!"

Come out, come out wherever you are," Big Tony said.

Big Tony gave off a big laugh. JoJo's men searched the room from top to bottom.

"Damn, he must've got away!"

"Don't worry. That little bitch couldn't have gone far," Tommy said.

"Maybe he went through here," Blue said as he pointed to the adjoining door. JoJo and his men pried open the door."

Michael climbed out of the bathroom window. He ran around to the front, and hopped in his car, and took off.
JoJo and his men saw the open bathroom window and ran to the front door. They saw Michael as he pulled out of the motel parking lot.

"Come on y'all, let's get that mutherfucka," JoJo said.

Jason's on the phone with Marsha.

"Where have you been?" Marsha said with an attitude.

"What do you mean, where have I've been? I didn't appreciate you sending that video to Stephanie."

"She needs to know about us!"

"I keep telling you, there is no us!"

"Yeah, right, tell that to yo dick!"

Jason laughed.

"Okay, well he heard that loud and clear now." Jason looked down at his penis.

"I can't believe you're going after your best friend's wife."

"Don't worry about what I'm doing, just know I won't be doing it with you anymore!"

Jason disconnected the call.

"That fuckin bastard." Marsha tossed her phone onto the couch.

Karen made several attempts to reach Michael. She paced back and forth.

"Will you please sit yo ass down!" One of the inmates said.

Karen glanced at the inmate and rolled her eyes.

"Don't start no shit with me!"

The inmate walked over and stood in front of her. Karen stood with her hands on her hips.

"What! Am I supposed to be scared?" Karen asked.

The inmate laughed.

"You will be sooner or later!"

The next morning, Karen walked into a cell that was occupied with another inmate on the other side of the cell.

Karen sat on her bed with her hands covering her face.

The inmate named Stacy was a white rough looking, tall, heavy-set female in her late thirties.

"Is this your first time?" Stacy asked.

Karen removed her hands.

"No, I have been in lockup a few times, but I have always made bail and was out within hours."

"What you in here for?"

"Embezzlement. What are you in here for?" Karen asked.

"Murder."

"Murder!" Karen said, shocked.

"Yes, I murdered my husband and his mistress."

"Wow!" Karen said.

Thirty minutes later, Karen and her cellmate walked into the cafeteria. Her cellmate showed her the ropes and gave her tips. The cellmate pointed to the first table.

"You see that table over there, you want to stay as far away from them as possible. Don't even make eye contact."

"Why?" Karen asked.

"They're a bad bunch of ladies who would easily cut your throat just for looking at them the wrong way.

Stacy pointed to another table.

"That table there, nothing but lesbians. They are going to try to approach you, and you will have to stand your ground with them."

Karen looked across the room and saw Susan and some other ladies. They locked eyes with each other.

"Do you know her?"

"Yes."

Across the room stood Susan and three other females.

"Hey." Susan pointed. "There goes that bitch right there!"

One of the inmates rubbed her hands together and then pointed across the room at Karen.

Karen and her cellmate Stacy stood in line to get lunch when one of Susan's buddies walked over and stood right behind Karen and Stacy. She cleared her throat. The ladies turned to look.

"Snitches get stitches, don't they Stacy?"

"Don't come over here with your threats, bitch." Stacy said.

Stacy stood in front of the cellmate with her back toward Karen.

"You need to take yo ass back over there with the rest of the losers!"

"You ain't gon always be with her, just remember that."

The ladies watched as the cellmate walked back over to where Susan and the other ladies sat. "They got it in for you so you need to be careful."

CHAPTER 9

The Church Sanctuary

Desmond stood at the altar. He watched as Candice walked toward him. The tears fell from his eyes as Candice approached the altar. He smiled as Candice came closer to him.

Candice wiped his tears and mouthed the words, "I love you."

Desmond took Candice's hand, and they turned and faced the Officiant.

"Family and friends, we are gathered here today to join in Holy Matrimony, Desmond Taylor and Candice Spencer."

Mrs. Taylor leaned over and whispered to her husband.

"He should have stayed with Stephanie. At least she has a job."

"Honey, not now," Mr. Taylor said.

"This contract is to be entered thoughtfully and seriously, and with a deep realization of its obligations and responsibilities." The marriage officiant said.

"I'm about to be sick," Mrs. Taylor said.

"If anyone knows why this couple should not be joined in holy matrimony, let him speak now or forever hold his peace.

Desmond looked back at his mom at the same time as his dad did. Mr. Taylor grabbed her hand just as she moved it.

Desmond bowed his head and closed his eyes.

"Candice, do you take Desmond to be your husband? Do you promise to love, honor, cherish, and protect him, forsaking all others, and holding only unto him forevermore?"

"I do!"

"Desmond, do you take Candice to be your wife? Do you promise to love, honor, cherish, and protect her forsaking all others, and holding only unto her forevermore?"

"I do!"

"Now for the rings. Candice and Desmond, please place the rings on each other's left hand and repeat after me. With this ring, I thee wed."

"With this ring, I thee wed," Desmond and Candice said in unison.

"By the power vested in me, I now pronounce you husband and wife! You may seal your vows with a kiss!"

The next day, the newlyweds prepared for their honeymoon. Candice grabbed the clothes and placed them into the suitcase. She grabbed the sexy nighty and held it up.

"I will most definitely need this," Candice said as she smiled.

Candice folded the nighty and placed it in a suitcase.

Desmond stood in the doorway.

"What do you have there?"

Candice jumped. "Damn. Desmond you scared me."

Candice closed the suitcase as Desmond walked up behind her. He grabbed her waist and kissed the back of her neck.

"I'm sorry!"

"No, you ain't."

Candice turned around and tapped Desmond on the shoulder and placed her arms around Desmond's neck.

"Baby, we are only going to be gone a week, I think you packed the entire room," Desmond said.

Candice grinned, "Look, a woman can never have too many clothes. There's an outfit for every occasion."

"Well, if things go the way I plan, you won't need half of what's in there," Desmond said as he grinned.

Desmond pulled her close to him and kissed her with so much passion."

Candice pulled away, "Hmm, we need to save some of this for later. We do have a plane to catch Mr."

Desmond grabbed the suitcase off the bed.

"Yes, we do, Mrs. Taylor," Desmond said as he smiled.

"Let's go before we miss our flight," Desmond said.

Jason sat at his desk looking over some paperwork with his accountant.

"Well, Jason, if you don't have any other questions, that should do it."

"Naw, I'm straight," Jason said as he put the paperwork back into the folder.

The accountant walked to the door as Marsha walked up. She moved aside to let him pass. Marsha walked in and stood as she eyed Jason.

"Why were you so rude the other day?"

"What are you talking about, and if I remember correctly, you were the one that was rude."

"Jason, do you think you can just use me whenever you like and toss me away when it's convenient for you?"

"Look, I made it clear the other day. I don't want anything to do with you. I don't know how to make this any clearer!"

Jason got up, walked over to Marsha, guided her out of his office, and shut the door behind him.

"What we had was good, but it has run its course."

Desmond and Candice's plane ride was smooth. They had just arrived to their hotel.

Candice walked in as Desmond rolled the luggage in.

"Oh baby, this is nice," Candice said as she looked around the hotel suite.

"Only the best for you, baby."

"You went all out didn't you?"

Desmond sat the luggage down, walked behind Candice, and wrapped his arms around her.

"You are now Mrs. Taylor the love of my life and the mother of my child, there is nothing I wouldn't do for you."

Candice smiled, "Oh baby, I love you!"

Candice turned to Desmond and kissed him just as his phone rang.

"Hold on for just a second," Desmond said as he pulled his phone out and answered.

"Yes, everything is perfect, thank you!"

Later that evening, Candice looked out at the beach. As Desmond walked up.

"This could not be more perfect."

"This is the beginning of a beautiful life together. Candice, I want to be the best husband and father to our child."

"And you will. You know, sometimes, I feel like I'm not deserving of this, having a good man who loves me."

"Well, believe it!"

"It's me and you, babe. I got you babe," Desmonds sang.

Candice laughed, "You know you can't sing."

Desmond took Candice's hand and twirled her around as he sang.

The next day, Candice sat on the couch with a magazine. Desmond walked in with a towel wrapped around his waist and flopped down next to Candice.

"How was your shower?"

"Great, what you got here?" He asked as he read out

loud, "How to have a healthy pregnancy. Is something wrong?"

"No, silly, I just want to take every precaution necessary since this is our first child."

"Yeah, I understand."

"You know, I was thinking about us getting a new life insurance policy. I know you already have one at work, but I was thinking about getting another for you and one for me with another Insurance Company?"

Desmond was surprised, "Where did that come from?"

"I've thought about it for a while and now that we're married and have a baby on the way. I think this is as good of a time as any, don't you think? I know you want the best for us, and if anything was to happen to you, me and the baby, would be left with nothing."

Desmond thought about what Candice said.

"How about we talk about this later."

Desmond stood up and removed his towel.

An hour later, Desmond and Candice were on the couch. Desmond pulled the magazine from up under him and looked over at her.

"Babe, if there was something wrong, you would tell me right?"

"Of course, I would."

Desmond leaned forward and kissed Candice.

"Ok, we have only a few more days, so how about we keep this honeymoon going?"

"You have not got enough yet?" Candice smiled.

"Pregnant sex is the bomb."

Candice laughed.

Later that night, Candice awakened and got out of bed. Desmond rolled over.

"Where are you going?"

"To the bathroom."

"Well hurry up, I'm ready for round two."

Inside the bathroom, Candice lifted the lid on the toilet and sat. She grabbed some tissue and wiped. She looked at the blood on the tissue and smiled as she glanced over at the bathroom door.

"Perfect!" Candice whispered.

"Baby, I'm ready," Desmond yelled.

Candice screams, "No! No!

Desmond jumped out of bed, he ran into the bathroom doorway.

"Still joking around I see."

Candice looked at Desmond as she held the bloody tissue.

"Oh my God! Baby, what's wrong."

Desmond rushed to Candice's side.

Candice screamed, "The baby! Oh no, my baby!"

Desmond and Candice made it to the ER in record time. Desmond paced back and forth in the lobby.

"Mrs. Taylor, what made you think you were pregnant?" The doctor asked as she applied gel to Candice's stomach.

"I took a home pregnancy test."

The doctor moved the transducer over her abdomen for a couple of minutes before looking at Candice.

"I'm sorry Mrs. Taylor, but that home pregnancy test gave you a false result. You're not pregnant. The blood you saw was just your menstrual cycle."

"No, that can't be true! You're wrong!"

"Again, I'm sorry. I can explain this to your husband if you like."

Candice yelled, "No! Don't you dare!"

"I'll tell him. Thank you, doctor," Candice said softly.

The doctor walked toward the door and turned around."

"You're free to leave whenever you're ready."
Desmond looked up and saw the doctor exit the examination room.

"Doctor! Doctor!" He ran toward her.
The doctor turned around and saw Desmond.

"Doc, how is she? How's the baby?"

"She will be fine. I will let her tell you the rest."
The doctor turned and walked away. Desmond pushed open the door slightly and stuck his head inside the room.

"Can I come in?" Desmond asked.
Candice shook her head, "Yes."
Desmond walked over to the bed and sat on the side. He hesitated to ask, "How's the baby?"
Candice looked Desmond in the eyes as the tears rolled down her face.
Candice began to cry, "We lost the baby."
Desmond pulled Candice closer to him. She lay her head against his chest as he rubbed her head.

"Shh... Don't cry, we can always try again."

CHAPTER 10

Five days later, Desmond and Candice visited the insurance company.

"How much coverage are you guys needing today?" The agent asked.

"I want enough that when it's time for me to go, my wife will not have to worry about anything."

Candice smiled as she rubbed the top of Desmond's hand.

"We want the same amount of coverage for the both of us." Candice chimed in.

The insurance agent looked over Desmond and Candice's information.

"I would suggest about 1.5 million."

"No, let's make it 2.5 million."

Desmond looked at Candice sideways and chuckled.

"Damn! I hope you're not planning to kill me."

"Don't be silly honey. Now, what would I do without you?"

Rodney walked out and saw Candice. He walked over to her and took a seat in front of her.

"What, no kiss or hug?" Candice asked.

"Sorry, but I'm not in a good mood today."

"What's wrong?"

"Do you really need to ask? You're busy playing house with this nigga, and I'm still in here!"

"Rodney, baby, don't be upset. I know he has someone working on your case."

"So when am I getting a new trial?"

"All I can tell you is that things are moving along, it won't be too much longer, trust me."

"Excuses is all I'm hearing for the last month or so."

78

"Look, don't get shitty with me, if you would have done what I told you to do, you wouldn't even be in here!'
Candice got up, walked over to the door, and waited to be led out.

Desmond stood by the counter as he talked to his mom on the phone.

"Thanks, mom, but that's not necessary. Candice seems to be doing just fine."

"Are you sure, son? How are you? After a loss like that, it's ok if you guys are not ok."

"I'm fine too. I'm back to work now. Staying busy. I just can't believe the baby is gone."
Desmond erupts into tears.

"I know it hurts but you got to stay strong. Candice needs you now more than ever."
Desmond wiped his eyes with his hand and took a deep breath.

"No, she doesn't. I hardly even see her anymore. She's always running this errand or that errand."
Desmond threw a hand in the air in frustration and paced.

"When I do, she never wants to talk about the baby. She says she's too tired. I don't know what to do!"
Desmond stopped.

"It's like... the baby never even existed."
Desmond's eyes grew big. He sat down.

"Well, I hate to ask this, but was she really pregnant?"

"What, I gotta go mom."

"Ok, baby, but please call me if..."
Desmond abruptly ended the call and made another call.

"Hello." Marcus said.

"I got a job for you. Can you meet me?"

Karen and her Cellmate were in their cell when the C.O. walked up.

"Yo Stacy you have a visit!" Carla the C.O. said.

"I got a visit?"

"Why do you look surprised?"

"Because I haven't filled out any visitor paperwork, so it must be my attorney," Stacy said.

"Well, that's what they told me."

Carla verified Stacy's info, and she guided Stacy down the hallway. Shortly after that, Karen heard the shower call over the loudspeaker for the inmates.

"Let me get in here and get this shower."

The cellmate next door yelled, "You ain't gonna wait for your girlfriend?"

"Damn bitch mind yo business," Karen yelled.

Karen put on her shower shoes, gathered some things together, and headed toward the showers.

As she made her way to the shower area, she noticed other inmates showering. She saw Susan and her posse. Susan gave her a dirty look and turned her head. Karen made sure not to stare at the inmates and quickly found a shower.

"Ooh, fresh meat! Did you like what you see beautiful? Do you need your back washed?"

Karen ignored the catcall. Karen rolled her eyes and exhaled slowly.

Karen said under her breath, "Let me hurry up and get out of here."

Karen began to lather her body with soap.

"Did you say something fresh meat?"

"Bitch you ain't all that. You could've just said thanks for the compliment or something instead of being rude. You gon learn, newbie."

"What's up with bitches in here not minding their own business?"

"Bitches minding their own business! Did you hear that?"

Several other inmates in that area comment back. Susan and her new friends heard the comments going back and forth.

Susan's cellmate quickly walked over, she spoke loudly as she walked up on Karen's left side.

Susan's cellmate said, "Yeah I agree I hate nosey bitches! I hate rude bitches, and snitching bitches the most."

Susan's cellmate's hand went up. Karen tried to block her, but she grabbed her arm. Someone from behind pulled a towel around her mouth. With Susan Cellmate's free hand, she slammed a shank deep into Karen's lower back as two other inmates jab her repeatedly on both sides. She knew she was being jumped by Karen's posse! Karen felt excruciating pain. She screamed, but they were muffled. Karen dropped to the floor. The room began to spin around. her vision became blurry as she lay in a puddle of blood.

Stacey walked into her cell when a cellmate across the way yelled.

"Yo, you need to check on ya girl. She went into the shower room alone."

"Shit!" Stacy yelled.

Stacey took off for the shower.

Stacey ran inside the shower to find Karen as she lay unconscious.

"Help! Somebody help!"

The guard ran in and quickly pulled out her walkie-talkie.

Desmond was sitting in the Insurance agent's office.

"What brings you back, Mr. Taylor. "I need to make a small change to my policy."

Desmond sat at the desk and reviewed the paperwork with the insurance agent.

"Is everything correct, Mr. Taylor?"

"Absolutely."

"Ok, I just need you to sign right here and initial there and it's done."

Desmond initialed the paperwork and passed the papers back to Tonya. Desmond looked at his phone clock.

"Thank you for taking care of this so quickly," Desmond said.

"My pleasure. Please let me know if you need anything else."

Desmond and Tonya stood and shook hands. They walked to the door. As Desmond left, he puts his phone to his ear.

"I'm on my way."

Desmond entered the King Ribs and removed his sunglasses. He saw Marcus Slay already seated with food on the table. Desmond approached Marcus.

"Oh, I see you started without me."

Marcus looked up, laughed, and wiped his mouth with a napkin.

"Hey, Des. Yeah, man, I'm sorry. It smelled so good. I couldn't wait."

Marcus gestured for Desmond to join him. Desmond shook his head, laughed, and sat at the table.

"Man, I said I was on my way," Desmond said jokingly.

"You want some of this?" Marcus pointed at his food.

"Naw, man. I'm just messing with you. I really need your help with something."

Desmond's face turned serious.

"It sounded really important on the phone."

"It is. It's about my wife."

"The old one or the new one?"

"Man, shut up! The new one," Desmond chuckled a little. His face turned serious again.

"I need you to find all the information you can on her. I have a suspicion, and I need to know if I'm right."

"You got it! I'll get on it right away. Well, after I finish these ribs and pay a visit to this guy named Trey at the Strip club."

Marcus picked up another rib. Desmond stood up and lightly slapped Marcus on the back.

"Thanks, man."

Desmond put on his sunglasses and left.

Stephanie pushed her grocery cart down the aisle when she stopped to check out the price of a large bottle of apple juice.

"Damn, that's high."

"I know," a customer said. "I was going to buy some myself, but when I saw the price, I put that shit back!"

Stephanie and the customer made small talk when a cart hit Stephanie's cart hard. Stephanie turned to look.

"Aw hell Naw! Did she just ram this cart into mine?"

"Damn! Do you know her? That seemed personal."

"I know who she is and she's barking up the wrong fuckin tree."

Stephanie ran after the lady, but she quickly disappeared.

Marcus Slay walked inside the strip club as one girl practiced her routine on the pole. Marcus spotted Trey Jones at a booth by the stage surrounded by women and drinks. As Marcus approached, Bone Crusher stepped in front of him.

"We're closed," Bone Crusher said.

"Uh, yes, I have a meeting with Trey Jones, "Marcus shouted over the music.

Bone Crusher looked at Trey, and Trey waved him over.

"He's good, Bones."

Bone Crusher stepped aside and walked over to the bar. Marcus went to the booth. Trey and his girls passed a blunt and offered it to Marcus. Marcus declined with a wave of the hand.

"Bones? What's that stand for?" Marcus asked.

"Bone Crusher. He goes where I go. Have a seat," Trey said.

Trey motioned for Marcus to sit in the empty spot on the end. Marcus sat. Trey dismissed the girls. Trey slapped one on the butt as she exited the booth.

"Oh, ok. Well, thanks for meeting me. As I said on the phone, I'm Marcus Slay, a private investigator for Rodney's case."

"Ah yeah, of course. Any friend of Rodney's is a friend of mine. But I'm not sure how I can help, man."

Trey stood and took a sip of his drink. He walked closer to the stage to flirt with the girl on the pole.

"Oh yeah, that's right, baby," Trey said.

Marcus got up and walked over to Trey.

"Can we go somewhere that's a little less noisy?"

"Sure man."

Trey took his drink to the office. Marcus and Bone Crusher followed.

Trey and Marcus walked in and closed the door. Bone Crusher stood guard on the outside of the room near the window that overlooked the club. Trey and Marcus sat in chairs opposite each other.

"Drink?"

"No thank you."

Trey refilled his glass and looked out the window at the topless girl.

"How much do you know about what went down that night?" Trey asked.

84

"I thought I was the one who was gonna be asking questions."

"Yeah, well, I can't tell you much. I wasn't even here. You really should just leave this alone."

"Oh yeah? Why is that? Don't you want to see your friend set free? I'm just trying to help."

Trey turned around to face Marcus.

"Of course, mayne. It's not like that. It's just you don't know how deep this goes and your snoopin' ain't helpin."

"So why did you agree to meet me?"

"Cause I know your kind. If I said no, you'd just think I'm hiding somethin."

"Are you?"

"Hell muthafuckin yeah! E'rybody's hidin sumthn. But this ain't that. Can't trust no one. Ya feel me."

"Ok, look. Whatever you tell me will be kept confidential. I'll keep your name out of it."

"I ain't tellin' you shit. I've said what I had to say."

"Trey put down his glass and opened the door."

"I have another meeting. It's time for you to leave. Bones, show this foo' to the door."

Trey put his hand in his pocket. He pulled out a flash drive and passed it to Marcus. Marcus continued out the door.

Trey whispered, "This from that night. Drive safe, and don't say I didn't warn you, mayne. Let this go," Trey said loudly.

Bones grabbed Marcus by the arm and led him away.

Bone Crusher pushed Marcus out the door.

"Hey!"

Bone Crusher closed the door.

Marcus got inside and took out the flash drive. He plugged it into his laptop.

"Holy shit!!"

85

Marcus called Desmond.

"Hey, I got something you're gonna want to see."

CHAPTER 11

Stephanie put her groceries in the trunk and shut it, and when she did, there stood Marsha.

"I don't know what you think you and Jason got going on, but believe me, he will never stop seeing me!"

"You need to get some help because you got some issues," Stephanie said.

"Yep, I sure do. And Jason is one of my issues."

"Well, that's something that you guys need to work out, and please, leave me out of it."

Marsha moved and stood directly in front of Stephanie.

"You need to stop seeing Jason or..."

Stephanie cut her off.

"Or what! Bitch? Don't threaten me, or you will get something that yo ass ain't bargaining for!"

Marsha said sarcastically, "We shall see."

Marsha walked over to her car, got in, and took off. Stephanie walked over to the driver's side and saw a long mark on her car.

"That fuckin bitch!" Stephanie yelled.

Stephanie took a picture of the damage and sent Jason a text message with the picture attached.

Jason sat at his desk talking to an employee when he got a text message.

"Tyler, can I get back to you. I need to handle something."

Jason picked up his phone.

"Hey, Jason, did you see what your little friend did to my car?"

"I did, and I am so sorry, Stephanie. I don't know why she would do something like that."

"Jason... are you serious right now? You don't think that you leaving her high and dry is the reason? I told you someone was going to get hurt behind y'all shit, and if she keeps this up, it will be her."

"I know she is upset with me, but for her to come after you, that's a whole different level."

"Exactly, you just thought you were having fun. Marsha has her feelings invested in you."

"I explained to her that our relationship wasn't like that... she knows this!"

"Yeah, well, when you put that dick on her, her heart said otherwise. This is serious Jason."

"I know, I will pay to have your car fixed."

"Damn it, Jason! I'm not talking about my car! **WHAT** are you going to do about **HER**?"

"I will talk to her again. Can you give me a few hours and everything should be resolved?"

"Jason, how well do you know this chick? Is she dangerous?"

"I know her well enough."

"Well, she rammed her grocery cart into mine before she damaged my car. She may be dangerous."

"Naw, she might be a little jealous, but she ain't dangerous."

"All I know is someone could get hurt, and if she keeps it up... just know it won't be me!"

"So, what are you saying?"

"I'm saying you better get your girl before she does a Lorena Bobbitt on you and relieves you of your manhood!"

"Man, I wish she would come at me like that."

"Well, you need to get her in check. Because I might catch a case if she comes at me again."

Jason said softly, "I'm sorry that Marsha came at you today. I'll make it up to you. How about a movie and dinner later?"

"That's a good start, but you need to have a heart-to-heart with her."

"I'll be at your place around 7:30. Chinese fine?"

"Chinese is perfect!"

Candice finished dinner for her in-laws. Desmond sat in the living room sipping his wine when the doorbell rang.

"Hey son, how's it going?" Mr. Taylor asked.

"It couldn't be better," Desmond looked over at his mom. "Hey mom."

Desmond kissed his mom on the cheek.

The Taylor's made their way into the kitchen to see Candice setting the table.

"Hello Candice, how are you?" Mrs. Taylor asked, trying to be nice.

"I'm good. How are you?"

"I'm good," Mrs. Taylor said as she sat down at the table and observed the dinner.

Mr. Taylor walked over and kissed Candice on the cheek. He hugged her as Mrs. Taylor looked at them, and rolled her eyes.

After everyone was seated, Mrs. Taylor spoke, "I was a little disappointed that your family didn't show up for the wedding. That's odd to me," Mrs. Taylor said as she bit into her fried potatoes.

"And why would that be odd to you? I told you my family and I wasn't close. We don't get along."

"You mean to tell me on your special day, you and your family couldn't put your differences aside?"

Candice said sarcastically, "My family is not like your

family. We don't fake at being loving and caring when we're not!"

"So what are you saying Candice? Do you think me and my husband are fake?"

Candice laughed, "If the shoe fits, I suggest you wear it!"

"Hey! That's my mom you're talking to! Desmond stood. "Candice, can I have a word with you in private!"

Desmond led the way to their bedroom.

Once they were inside, Desmond grabbed Candice by the arm.

"What the hell is your problem! How could you disrespect my parents like that?"

"Me! What about your nosey ass mother! She's always in my business. She needs to mind her own fuckin business!"

"You know, you have been acting differently after losing our baby. I know this has been hard for you, but damn..."

Candice cuts Desmond off.

"But damn, what? I'm your wife. You should be defending me, not your mother."

"I will always defend you when you're right, but right now, you are dead wrong!"

Candice said sarcastically, "I see, momma's boy!"

"Momma's boy!"

"You heard me!"

"I'm gonna act like you didn't just say that. You have no idea how many fuckin' times I've stood up for you."

"What are you talking about?"

Desmond's and Candice's raised voices could be heard in the kitchen.

Mrs. Taylor pushed her chair back from the table.

"Where are you going?"

"I'm not going to sit here and be disrespected like that in my son's house! Who does she think she is?"

"His wife, that's who! This is her house too. What did you expect, attacking her family?" Mrs. Taylor folded her arms.

"I can't believe you sat there and let her talk to me that way. Thank God, our son stepped in and...

Candice and Desmond walked back into the kitchen.

"And what!"

"And put your ass in your place!"

"You know you brought this shit on yourself. Even though Desmond won't say it, but you're the one always putting me down, aren't you?"

Candice bent down and got in Mrs. Taylor's face.

"What kind of mother are you?"

Mrs. Taylor rose from the table. "The kind of mother that will put my foot so far up your ass, little trashy ass girl...!"

Desmond leaped in between the two women.

"Momma! I think it's time for you to go."

Mr. Taylor jumped up from the table.

"I agree!"

Candice swiped the open wine bottle off the table and took a big swig. Mrs. Taylor looked appalled as Candice narrowed her eyes.

"Yeah, I think that's best," Candice said.

Mr. Taylor ushered Mrs. Taylor to the door. Desmond followed them.

Mrs. Taylor shouted, "If you ask me, my son could do a lot better than you! Maybe that's why you lost your baby," Mrs. Taylor pointed to the wine bottle, "If you were really pregnant!"

Candice shouted, "Nobody's asking you!"

Desmond quickly closed the front door and returned to Candice. He just stopped and looked at her.

"Well... that went well," Candice said sarcastically.

Desmond looked dumbfounded, "What the fuck has gotten into you?"

Candice laughed and took another swig.

"What? The old geezer had it coming."

"Don't you ever talk to my mother like that again! You know I have never laid a hand on a female, but right now, you make me want to knock the fuck out of you!"

"Whatever. She started it."

"You know it's not too late to get an annulment, right?"

Candice put the bottle down on the counter and went upstairs.

Desmond screamed, "Fucccccck!!!"

Desmond pulled his phone from his pocket and listened to his voice message from Marcus.

The next day, Desmond walked in and looked around for Rodney. He sat down at a table and took out his writing tablet and pen. Desmond tapped his pen on the table several times before Rodney walked through the door and took a seat a the table.

"Good afternoon, Rodney."

They shook hands.

"Hey, good to see you. I am sorry you had to wait, but you switched up the day you usually come."

"No problem."

"So, what's up?"

"The investigator that I have been working on your case did get a positive lead. Looks like people were willing to help as long as their name stays clear."

"Yes! Yes!"

Rodney did a fist pump in the air.

"I know it's not a ton of new information, but I wanted to let you know there is progress being made."

"It's good to know something is going on."

"I also wanted to check back just to see if you thought of any other information or anyone else that could help your case?"

"No, I gave you all the names I had, but uh, how was your honeymoon?"

Desmond looked at him sideways.

"How do you know I went on a honeymoon. I never mentioned that to you?"

"All man, my girl told me. I just wanted to hear about some more good news that's all. I wanted to see what it is like to be you."

Desmond gave Rodney a sharp look.

You know, a free man living life, and honeymooning.

Desmond had a puzzled look on his face as he gathered his things up to leave.

"I'll be in touch," Desmond said as he stood to leave.

CHAPTER 12

 $\mathbf{F}$ **rank** and Ramar sat at the table. The waiter walked over with two drinks. The waiter set one drink in front of Frank and the other drink in front of Ramar.

"Don't you think it's a little early for margaritas?"
Frank sipped his drink.

"Hmm, it ain't never too early with all the stress I'm under. Shid a bitch need two more just to relax."
Frank waved the waiter over.

Ramar laughed, "You crazy!"

"I'm serious… this witness protection shit got me all out of my routine."
Frank took another sip.

"I can't go out because I could be followed. I can't call anyone because my phone might be tapped. Hell, I might as well have Covid."

"That ain't funny."

"Well, that's how I feel. I'm the one supposed to be protected, but I feel like I'm back on lockdown again. Make that make sense."
The waiter walked up.

"You gentlemen ready to order?"
Frank said as he flirted with the waiter, "I'll take you and another one of these, handsome."
Frank rubbed his hand against the waiter. The waiter walked away with a smile.

"You know you need to stop."

"And a bitch ain't been laid."
Frank took another drink.

"They still haven't caught this bastard, huh?"

"No and who's to say he ain't out there watching me right now."

"Look, just know I got you. I ain't going to let nothing happen to you."

Michael sat on the bed as he smoked a blunt. His phone vibrated, so he picked it up and read his message.

"Don't think I ain't gone find yo bitch ass! My boys on every block, you can't hide nigga!"

Michael tossed his phone and took another puff of the blunt.

"You know what, fuck it, I ain't about to be hiding out like some bitch."

Michael grabbed his keys and left the room. He pulled up to the stoplight, he bopped his head to the music.

"All hell yeah! Some muthafucking tacos about to hit the spot."

Michael pulled into the lot and park. He opened the door and was about to get out when he saw Frank.

Frank and Ramar hugged each other.

"Thank you for coming, I really needed this."

"You know I got you, whatever you need."

"I need that fine ass waiter in there to come home with me."

They both laughed.

"You know he ain't yo type."

"Bitch, with the stress I'm under, you would be my type right about now.

Ramar laughed. "You a damn fool. You sure you don't want me to take you home?"

"No, my Uber is around the corner."

Michael sat in his car and watched, "Well, the dead has arisen, literally."

The Uber pulled up.

"See, here he is now, and he cute, maybe I can give him an extra tip."

Ramar opened the back door.

"You need to take yo drunk ass home and get some sleep. I'll text you tomorrow."

"Ok, love you bitch."

"Love you too," Ramar said.

Ramar closed the door and the Uber drove off.

Michael started the engine and followed behind the Uber.

"Oh, this shit is too easy."

Michael parked and watched as Frank ran around to the back of the house.

As Frank entered the witness protection home, he walked into the kitchen when two police officers stood at the entrance.

Frank jumped.

"Oh, Shit!"

"What part of witness protection don't you understand? You're under protection for a reason," The first officer said.

"You have just put us in jeopardy. What if the person we are trying to protect you from saw you?' The second officer said.

The first officer said, "If you can't follow the rules, I will suggest you be taken off the program."

"I'm sorry, it won't happen again."

Later that night, Michael parked across the street from the witness protection home and walked around to the back, turned the knob to the back door, and to his surprise, it opened.

Michael slowly walked inside and looked around. He pulled out his gun and attached the silencer. He scanned the kitchen and then the living room where he saw two police officers as they watched TV.

"Aw shit! Did you see that nonsense?" The first officer asked.

The second police officer looked up to see Michael and reached for his gun, but Michael dead's him, and then dead's the other officer.

Frank was upstairs in his room when he heard a loud noise. He ran to the bedroom door and stood still listening for any sound.

Michael heard footsteps so he made his way to the stairs.

Michael made his way to the first bedroom door and slowly opened it. He searched the closet, under the bed, and walked out. He made his way to the second bedroom, where he slowly turned the knob with one hand and held the gun in the other. He scanned the room and then walked over to the closet. He stood there for several minutes before he yanked the doors open.

Frank hid back up against the closet wall. He blended in with the darkness. Michael searched the closet and came up empty-handed. He turned around and looked at the bed.

Michael said angrily, "I know you're here, Frank, so bring yo little ass out from under the bed!"

Michael moved over to the side of the bed. He got down on one knee, pulled the sham up, and looked under the bed. When he rose he saw the window, it was up. He rushed over and looked out. He rushed out of the room, downstairs, and out the front door.

Seconds later, Frank eased out of the closet and walked over to the window. He stood back and saw Michael outside.

Michael ran to the sidewalk and looked up and down the street. He dashed across the street to his car. He pulled off and sped down the street as he looked on each block and corner for Frank.

Frank quietly made his way downstairs where he saw the dead police officers. He ran and locked the front door and pulled out his phone.

"Oh my God!" Frank yelled as he nervously dialed Detective Morris's number.

"Pick up, pick up, please!" Frank said, Frantically.

Detective Morris reached over and grabbed his phone off the nightstand.

Twenty minutes later, Police cars surrounded the witness protection home as Frank was escorted out of the house and into an unmarked black police car.

At the police precinct, Frank sat at Detective Morris's desk.

"Okay, Frank, how do you know it was Michael?"

"After Michael ran out the front door, I saw him out on the sidewalk. I watched as he drove away."

"How did he find you?"

"I did something I shouldn't have done. I snuck out and met up with a friend of mine. Michael must have seen us."

Detective Morris hit his fist on the desk.

"Damn it, Frank! I'm sorry, but we can't put you in witness protection again. You caused two deaths because you disobeyed orders!"

"I am so sorry, but what if he finds me?" Frank cried.

Detective Morris, shook his head, "My advice to you is to get a gun to protect yourself."

At Methodist Hospital, Karen lay on the gurney as the EMT and Nurses rushed her down the hallway.

An hour later, a man and woman run to the front desk at Methodist Hospital.

"Excuse me Ms., my sister was brought here, where is she?"

"Ma'am, I need you to calm down!"

The sister yelled, "Don't tell me to calm down! She was brought here. They said she had been stabbed, where is she?"

Brett, Karen's brother leaned on the counter, "Ma'am I'm sorry! My sister is just upset, can you please check to see if my sister is here?"

"What is her name?"

Sara slammed her fist on the counter.

"Her name is Karen!" Sara said.

One of the ER clerk looked at Sara and rolled her eyes.

"Karen Jamison," Brett said.

"Thank you!" She mumbled, "At least someone has some sense."

"I know things haven't been easy for you all with the pandemic and all. Thank you for your service," Brett said.

"That's what they get paid to do," Sara blurted out.

The ER clerk rolled her eyes and kept typing on the computer keyboard.

"Yes, it looks like your sister was rushed into emergency surgery, suffering from multiple stabs," Sara screamed as the tears flowed.

"When can we see her?"

"I'm sorry, but our policy doesn't allow visitors past the waiting room due to the pandemic and besides, she is in police custody." The ER clerk blurted out.

"What! So we can't see our sister. You mean to tell me she has to go through this alone?" Sara shouted angrily.

"I'm sorry, but that is the policy." The ER clerk said.

"You can take your policy and stick it up your ass!" Sara yelled.

Brett wrapped his arm around Sara as they walked to the guest area. Brett and Sara sat down. A nurse walked to the nurse's station and set the clipboard on the counter.

"What's going on?" Nurse Rachel asked as she looked over to the guest area.

Nurse Rachel walked over to Brett and Sara. Nurse Rachel was surprised, "Brett, Sara!"

"Rachel!," Brett stood.

"What are you all doing here? Is everything ok?"

"You work here?" Brett asked.

"No, I'm just filling in while we're in this pandemic. So what's going on, is it Aunt Jenny?"

"No, it's Karen," Brett said.

"What happened?"

Sara jumped up and pointed to the clerk.

"She won't let us see our sister."

"She's upset," Brett chimed in.

"You damn right! And so should you!" Sara shouted.

"Ok, give me a sec, I'll see what I can find out." Rachel walked over to the nurse's station.

Brett looked at Sara, "You have to calm down, they're doing all they can under a lot of stress."

Rachel walked back over to Brett and Sara.

"Ok, so she is in surgery now. It's very serious, but as soon as I know more, I will call you."

"She was jumped in the shower. Who would do something like this?" Rachel said.

"She's in prison, what do you expect. Those people are savages."

"Look, go home! I'll let you know if anything changes."

100

CHAPTER 13

Desmond looked at the files on his desk.

What am I missing?

The light on his office phone blinked. Desmond put the phone to his ear.

"Marcus Slay is here to see you," Cynthia said.

"Oh, good, send him in."

Marcus walked through the door with a small package in his hand. Desmond stood.

"I hope whatever you got in there is bigger than it looks. We need a miracle to reopen this case."

"Oh, trust me, it's big!"

Marcus walked over to the desk and gave Desmond the package. Desmond opened the package and pulled the flash drive out.

"What's this?"

"This my friend is a copy of the video footage from the club on the night of the murder."

"What! How'd you get it?" Desmond got excited.

Marcus folded his arms and smiled.

"Trey, from the club."

Desmond plugged the flash drive into his computer and opened the file as Marcus sat.

"Come on, come on, I don't want to be here all day! Okay, okay, here we go. So, what am I looking for?"

"Don't worry, it's a clip of the relevant security footage. Fast-forward to 6.80 and hit play."

Desmond fast-forwarded, he hit play, and watched the video clip. After a few seconds, a huge smile developed on his face.

"Wow! Yes! Finally the break we need. I can't believe this is all they had on him."

"I knew you'd like that."

"Man! You don't know how badly I needed this."

"Well, if this video is any indication, then it looks like ya boy really is innocent."

"It's definitely a start in the right direction. I think I almost have enough to convince a judge to grant us an appeal."

"Cool. I'm going to call in a favor from my contact at IMPD. I wanna see what other evidence they have, if any."

"Thanks, man."

Desmond and Marcus stood up, shook hands, and walked to the door.

"I'll keep the original in my safe until the trial. You can keep that copy."

"Alright, sounds good."

Marcus headed through the door. Desmond returned to his desk.

Marcus jogged and stopped on the bridge. Alexandria Rodriguez jogged from the opposite direction and stopped beside him. Marcus checked his vitals on his watch. Alex started to jog in place and then stretched her legs. Marcus looked over the side of the bridge.

"Officer Rodriguez. How is IMPD treating you?"

"Small talk. Really, Marcus?"

They faced each other.

"I'm just wondering how you are, but it's cool. Did you bring the file?"

"Yeah, I brought it and I'm good. You know I could get in real trouble for this though."

"You'll be helping free an innocent man. Isn't that what's most important?"

102

"He may not be guilty of *this* crime, but I doubt he's innocent."

"C'mon, Alex. You know our history. I would never let this fall back on you."

Marcus gave Rodriquez those sad puppy dog eyes look. Alex sighed and leaned up against the bridge. She pulled a flash drive out of the pocket of her leggings. She placed it in Marcus's hand.

"I know," Alex said.

They held hands for a few long seconds. Alex pulled her hand away.

"I gotta go. That is a copy of what we have on Rodney including the juror list. It should give you everything you need."

"Thank you, Alexandria."

Alex jogged off. Marcus admired her form briefly, then he turned and jogged away in the opposite direction.

Karen was out of surgery and had been taken to her room. There was a police officer stationed outside of her door.

Rachel entered the room and spoke to the nurse on duty.

"Hi, how is she?" Rachel asked.

They stepped away from Karen's bed. "She's lost a lot of blood."

Rachel looked over Gina's shoulder, "Aw, I see she's awake."

"She's in and out of it. She is very lucky, but she is in serious condition."

Looking at the paper in Gina's hand.

"I have her emergency contact list so her info can be placed on her board here in the room. Her family keeps calling, but she is in police custody so they can't visit."

"Ok, I'll call them immediately as soon as I come back

from the restroom."

"Oh, no problem I'll make the call," Rachel insisted.

"Oh, thank you!"

Gina exited the room. Rachel moved over to Karen's bed.

"Hey, Karen, it's me Rachel."

Karen opened her eyes. She gave Rachel a slight smile.

"I'm so glad to see you. Will you call Michael and tell him what happened and that I'm here?"

Rachel took out her cell phone, "What's his number"

Karen rattled off his number, and Rachel dialed.

"Hello."

"Hey, this is Rachel, Karen's cousin. She gave me your number to call you. I have some good and bad news."

Rachel told Michael what had taken place, then placed the phone up to Karen's ear.

"Hey babe," Karen spoke softly.

"You just hang in there. I will get you out of there, I promise. Did Susan do this to you?"

"She was there, but I didn't see who all stabbed me. I was jumped by some of the chicks in her click.

"Oh, she was in on it, I know it. I'm so sorry Karen I never thought this and the Frank stuff would spiral out of control like this."

"What do you mean, did you take care of the issue with him?"

"No, I was in the process, but I had to take out some officers, and he got away. Sorry to lay this on you now, but he got away."

Rachel motioned to Karen to hurry up.

"Rachel says we gotta go. She doesn't want anyone to pop in and see me using her phone. Love you."

"Love you and I'll be in touch. Let me talk to Rachel real quick."

Jason's phone rang as he parked. He saw it was Marsha and ignored her call again. Jason picked up his phone.

"Let me stop this right now and put this on silent."
Jason changed the settings on his phone. He grabbed the food and flowers from the car before walking up to Stephanie's door.
Talking into Jason's voicemail. "I know you're not busy.... you're gonna keep ignoring me now that Stephanie is paying your kiss ass some attention."
Marsha called Jason again, and it rang and rang, then it went to his voice mail. When she called again, it went directly to voicemail.

"Oh, you don't want to be disturbed, huh? Well, let's see how you like it when I show up on your doorstep, bitch!"
Marsha grabbed her car keys, purse, and headed out the door. She arrived at Jason's, but his car wasn't there. She got out of her car and pounded on the door. He still didn't answer, so after a few minutes, she left. She headed over to see if he' was at Stephanie's place.

Stephanie opened the door, and all she saw was a beautiful dozen yellow roses!

"Hello!" Jason said.
Jason peeked around the roses and saw Stephanie's beautiful smiling face. She took them and stared at them.

"These are absolutely gorgeous. I've never had yellow roses before."

"These symbolize friendship, and since we're starting over and building a different type of friendship and bond, I thought these would be perfect."
Jason set the food down and Stephanie put the flowers down and walked towards Jason and they embraced. Stephanie looked up at Jason.

"I never knew that. Are you pulling my leg?"

"No, it's true. You can look it up after this."
Jason leaned in and kissed Stephanie on the lips. Then he quickly pulled away and playfully spoke fast.
"We need to eat before the food gets cold."
Stephanie looked at Jason with a shocked look on her face and rolled her eyes and laughed.

Later that evening, Marsha pounded on the door of Stephanie's home.
"Hellooo, anybody home?"
Jason opened the door with Stephanie on his heels. Jason spoke through the security door.
"What are you doing here? I can't believe even you would stoop this low?"
What did you expect? You ignored my calls, so I wanted to show you I won't be ignored!"
"Woman, you've lost your mind!"
"Have I? One minute we're together and..."
Jason cut Marsha off.
"You kept throwing yourself at me. I've explained this to you until I was blue in the face that there is no me and you."
"You can't just treat women like a toy Jason."
"I'm sorry you feel this way. I've apologized more than once, but you need to own up to your actions."
"Oh, you are blaming me now."
"It was consensual sex that's all it was. I was upfront with you. You thought you could change my feelings."
"No, that's not all it was, and you know it. Why did you tell me you loved me if it was just sex?"
"Get out of here."
Jason shut the door in Marsha's face. When she left, she noticed Stephanie's neighbor looking at her. Marsha yelled at him.

"Who are you, the neighborhood watch! I suggest you take yo' ass and go in the house and watch something or somebody else, nosey ass!"
Marsha walked down the sidewalk to her car. She reached for her keys, grabbed the knife instead, turned, and walked towards Jason's and Stephanie's cars.

"Both of y'all bitches got me messed up! I don't know who the fuck you think I am Jason!" Marsha spoke loudly.
The neighbor went into the house, but continued to watch Marsha from the window.

"I went out of my way to please you, and this is how you do me!"
Marsha again plunged the knife into both driver-side tires. She headed towards Stephanie's car.

"And you man stealing ho', I got something for you!"
Marsha looked around for something to break a window when she saw a large stone near the bushes.

"You gon' learn tonight not to mess with my man again."
She picked up the large stone with two hands and threw it into Stephanie's windshield. She calmly walked back to her car, got inside, and drove away.
Jason and Stephanie looked at each other after they heard the glass shatter. Jason muted the remote.

"What was that?" Jason asked.

"It sounded like glass shattering. Probably some teens up to no good again."

"I'll go see; you stay there."
Jason walked to the window and saw nothing but darkness. He opened the front door and saw Stephanie's windshield was shattered.

"What is it Jason, is it glass?" Stephanie asked.

"Oh, it's glass alright. Your windshield is completely

shattered."

Jason continued to look at the cars and noticed the flat tires.

"WHAT? My WINDSHIELD? Why would my windshield be...?"

Jason cut her off, "I think we need to head outside; the tires are flat too."

"Tires flat! My tires were just aired up... wait a minute. I know that bald-headed, crazy-ass Marsha..."

Jason put on his shoes, "Hey, slow down. You said yourself it could be some teens up to no good."

Stephanie slipped on her shoes, "That was before it was my windshield! There is a difference between breaking a glass bottle and a windshield."

"I guess you're right, and the fact that all the tires are flat doesn't help."

"Tires! Oh, hell no Jason, if that bitch did this, I'm going to strangle her. What the hell did you do to her?"

"I have told you, again and again, nothing. I told her we were not a thing."

Jason and Stephanie walked outside and looked at the windshield and tires. Jason walked around Stephanie's car and noticed the other tires were slashed.

"You may have to file a claim on this one. That windshield is done for."

"Damn!! This ain't real right now!"

Stephanie walked over to Jason.

"What the Hell! That does it. She fuckin with the wrong one. She doesn't know me, but she gon learn tonight."

Stephanie is pacing back and forth behind Jason as he observes the tires.

"Take me to that ho's house right now!!!! I'm bout to get some Vaseline and beat her muthafuckin ass!!!"

"Calm down, Foxy Brown! I'm not taking you to

Marsha's house. But I am going take you inside so you can call the police and file a claim."

"Taking me inside won't fix this mess, Jason!"

CHAPTER 14

Rachel walked into Karen's hospital room.

"How do you feel?"

"I feel much better."

"You know they're transporting you back to jail tomorrow morning."

"No, I can't go back there. I need a favor, a huge favor." Later that evening. Rachel handed Michael a doctor's coat with credentials.

"I'll get the guard to remove the cuffs while you pretend to evaluate her movement up and down the hall."

"What happens if he doesn't do it?"

"He will, but you have five minutes to get her out of the hospital. I will occupy the guard while you and Karen slip out."

"What if someone sees us?" Michael asked.

"Damn, stop being so fuckin negative. Take the stairs to the basement and follow the red arrows. It will lead you up some stairs to an exit right by the parking garage."

"Is she in any condition to do all of this?"

"No, not really, but it's this, or she goes back to jail. I will have some supplies and medicine ready for you to take that will help her with the pain."

Rachel talked to the guard as Michael dressed as a doctor, walked into Karen's room.

"Her cuffs need to be removed for just a few minutes. The doctor needs to check her mobility," Rachel said.

"You know I can't do that. I have strict orders not to remove her cuffs."

Desmond pulled his car up to the front door. Desmond and Candice exited the car. Desmond handed his keys to the valet. He opened the door.

Desmond and Candice entered and walked up to the hostess counter.

"Welcome to Ruth Chris. Do you have a reservation?"

"Yes, Taylor."

"Party of 2?" The hostess asked.

Desmond nodded. The hostess led them to a secluded booth. They sat down, and the hostess gave them menus.

"Your server will be right with you."

"Thank you," Desmond said.

Candice looked at the menu.

"You've been really quiet these last couple of days since you and my mom got into it," Desmond said.

Candice rolled her eyes at the mention of his mom. She continued to study the menu.

"Are you seriously going to keep giving me the silent treatment? It's been almost a week!"

"What do you want me to say, Desmond?" Candice calmly asked.

The server appeared and placed the bread on the table.

"Hi, my name is Luis, and I will be your server tonight. Would you like to hear the specials?"

Candice flirted with the server, "Luis? Well, yes, I would like that very much."

Desmond cleared his throat.

"Can you give us a minute, Luis?"

"Of course."

Luis checked on another table. Candice slumped in her seat and folded her arms.

"Candice, I brought you here tonight so we could try to

111

get back on track. Everything has been off with us lately. I miss you."

"So, you thought instead of talking to me, you would just buy me an expensive ass dinner, and everything will be ok."

"That's not what I'm saying. I just want to get things back to the way they were."

"Yeah, by throwing money at me! Lucky for you, I'mma bout to order the fuck outta this menu."

Candice sliced some bread as server-Luis returned.

"Are you ready to order?"

"Yep!"

Frank was on his phone talking to Ramar.

"Thanks for helping me out with the clothes and giving me a place to stay."

"Don't mention it, I'm sorry it's the least I could do, but after what just happened at the protection house."

"I can't believe this happened to me."

"I can't either."

"I'm pulling up in a blue Malibu," Frank said.

Ramar peeped through the blinds from his window and saw the Malibu pull up and park behind his car. Ramar walked downstairs to the back door and opened it.

Stephanie pulled into her driveway after picking her car up from the shop. Jason pulled in right behind her and met her at the front door. He could tell she was still pissed about her car.

"Steph, I know you're still angry with me about the other day, but try to understand why I didn't want you to tell the police about Marsha."

"I just don't get it when it comes to you and that nutty Nancy."

Jason chuckled and then he tried to hide his smile. He put

his hands around her shoulders.

Stephanie rolled her eyes as they walked through the door. Stephanie closed the door, locked it, and turned around to Jason's face as he met hers.

"Look, I don't want to ever see a black man or woman arrested for something that has not physically harmed someone. I will talk to her and have her reimburse you for the damages. Will that make you feel better?"

Stephanie softened up a little. " I don't know."

"I know something that will help."

"Oh really."

Jason kissed Stephanie and she kissed him back. Stephanie moaned and put her arms around Jason's neck. She pulled him closer. Jason gripped Stephanie's breasts and massaged his way to her nipples. Stephanie unbuttoned her shirt. Jason's tongue circled one of her nipples, and then the other.

Stephanie moaned with each touch of his tongue. She reached for his shirt, pulled it over his head as she rubbed his chest, and grasped his nipple in between her fingers.

Jason groaned at the touch of Stephanie's hands.

"Damn Steph, I want you to." He said softly into her ear.

Jason picked her up, carried her over to the sofa, and kissed her. Just as he lay her down, his phone rang. Jason picked up his phone off the table. He didn't recognize the number, but he still answered.

"Hello."

"Jason! I'm so glad you answered!"

"What the hell, Marsha! Why did you call my phone?

Stephanie sat up after hearing that Marsha was on the phone."

"Jason, someone is trying to break in my house! They're at the back door!"

"What the fuck are you calling me for? Call the police and let them handle it."

Stephanie glared at Jason, waiting for his conversation with Marsha to be over so they could finish what they started.

"Jason! Jason! Are you listening to me? I'm so scared!"

"Yes, I hear you, did you call the police?"

Stephanie heard "police" and motioned to Jason to put the phone on speaker. As Jason questioned her motion, Steph reached and pressed the speaker button.

"No, I called you first. I figured you could come over..."

"You figured wrong bitch! This ain't 911."

Jason tried to cover the phone to keep Marsha from hearing Stephanie but he was too late. He took the phone off speaker instead and put it to his ear.

"Jason, you better tell her to mind her business because this is serious. I need your help. Please come over. Please!"

"Why should I come to help you after what you did to our cars? Do you know how much damage you have caused?"

"I know, and you are right. I'll pay to have your car fixed. I just need your help, please. Oh my God, they are banging on the front door now!"

"Call 911! I'll be there soon."

Marcus slid the flash drive in and scrolled down for the list of the jurors. He searched for their addresses as he made several notes on his notepad. Then he removed the flash drive.

Candice picked at her salad. Desmond broke the silence.

"I finally got a major break in the Rodney case, and I was hoping to celebrate with you."

Candice sat up with interest.

"You did? What kind of break?"

"I can't say too much about it yet, but this could really be the thing that sets him free."

"Oh my God! We knew you could do it!"

Candice smiled from ear to ear as if in a daydream.

"We?"

"Yeah, uh. Me and Trina."

"Oh. Well, I appreciate your enthusiasm, but I haven't done anything yet."

"But you ARE making progress, right?"

"Yes."

"That's all I needed to hear! Can we go? I need to run some errands in the morning, and it's getting late."

"But you've barely eaten? I thought we were going to celebrate."

"I'm ready to go now."

Desmond signaled the server and paid for the meal. Candice left the booth and headed outside.

Desmond met up with her at the valet. He put his arm around her waist as they waited for the car.

The next morning, Candice walked from the bathroom over to the dresser, put on her earrings. Desmond was still in the bed. He turned over and looked at Candice.

"Good morning!"

"Morning."

"I thought we could sleep in this morning."

"I told you, I had some errands to run."

"You look nice. Where are you going?"

"Do I question you when you leave this house?" She said with an attitude.

"Where is this attitude coming from? I just want to spend some quality time with my wife."

"Well, I have things to do."

"I don't like being at odds with you. I'm doing everything I know to make things right with us, but I can't do this by myself."

Candice grabbed her purse, looked at Desmond, and walked towards the door.

"I'll see you later."

Candice walked out. Desmond eased out of bed and walked into the kitchen. He poured a cup of coffee and walked over to the table, and sat down. He picked up his phone and read a text message from Marcus.

"Hey, going to see one of the jurors today. I'll keep you posted."

Desmond typed back.

"Cool!"

Desmond pulled up Candice's name on his phone and hit the phone button. The phone went to voicemail.

"This me Candice, leave a message and I'll get back to you."

Desmond looked at the phone and then lay it down on the table.

The door opened, Rodney walked in and sat down in front of Candice.

Candice smiled, "Hey baby!"

"You look damn good. You all dressed up for me?"

"Who else would it be for?"

"Well, you are married."

"Yeah, just in name sake only."

"Oh really!" Rodney grinned.

"Yes, really, and I wanted to be the first to tell you the good news."

"And what would that be?"

"There's a break in the case, I don't know all the details, but things are about to change, baby."

"So your bitch ass husband is finally doing some work on my behalf."

"Yes, and we are that much closer to being together." Candice removed one of her shoes and touched Rodney under the table. Rodney tilted his head over and looked under the table. Candice opened her legs.

Rodney licked his lips, "Hmm damn."

"We stick to the plan ok?"

"I got you."

Marcus knocked three times before the front door opened. "Lorraine Johnson."

"Can I help you, sir?"

"Hello Ma'am, are you Mrs. Lorraine Johnson?"

"Who's asking?"

"I'm sorry, my name is Marcus Slay. I'm a private investigator. Can I have a moment of your time?"

"Sure."

Lorraine opened the door for Marcus to enter.

"Would you like something to drink?"

"No, ma'am, I'm good. I am here to talk with you about a trial you were involved in."

Lorraine Johnson shook her head.

"That figures."

"So you already know what trial I'm talking about?"

"Yes, I have only been in one jury pool, and that was a joke. They convicted that young man with no real evidence."

"So, are you saying that you didn't believe he was guilty?"

"Of course not. Everyone was voting in his favor until we got a visit from some men and the judge."

"Wait a minute. So you are saying the judge and some men told you how to vote?"

"Yes, they told us it would be in our best interest to all vote the same way. I heard a couple of the jurors had been paid to convince us to vote him guilty."

"Are any of those jurors' names on this list?"

Marcus pulled a list out of his jacket pocket and handed it to Lorraine.

Twenty minutes later, Marcus sat in his car. He pulled out his cell and dialed.

"What's up my man?"

"Man, you are not going to believe what I just heard?" Desmond sounded excited.

"Hit me with it!"

"I am getting ready to visit two of the jurors that were supposedly paid to convict Rodney, and guess what... the judge was involved."

"No way!"

CHAPTER 15

The officer removed the cuffs from Karen's wrist.

"There you go, Doc."

"Thank you, officer!"

The officer walked to the door, he looked back at the doctor.

"Excuse me, doctor"

Michael hesitated, " Yes, officer.

"How long will this take?"

"We need to test her strength and mobility, so I think five minutes would be a good effort, don't you think nurse?"

"Yes, we don't want to overwork her too much," Rachel said.

"Ok, I'm going to grab a coffee," The officer said.

The door closed. Rachel slowly opened the door and peeked out.

"Ok, he's gone. You have to go now!"

Michael helped Karen off the bed.

"I got you, baby."

"Ok, it's all clear. Do you remember what I told you?" Rachel asked.

"Yes."

Rachel held the door open while Karen took steps.

"You're doing great, Karen!"

Michael and Karen walked to the exit door. Michael looked around, he opened the door, and Karen walked through.

"Michael, I don't know if I can make it any further."

"Karen, we have to, if not, this place will be on

lockdown and they will be looking for you. We are almost to the exit."

Once they made it to the exit, Michael noticed blood on Karen's gown.

"Oh shit! Babe, you're bleeding!"

Michael grabbed Karen up in his arms and proceeded out the door to the parking garage.

Michael parked his car right by the entrance. Instead of taking the elevator to the second floor, he continued to carry Karen up the stairs.

"Oh my God! We made it babe."

Michael and Karen exited the parking garage just as they saw police officers run into the hospital.

"Damn, that was close," Michael said.

"Babe, where are we going?"

Michael looked over and saw Karen holding her side. He reached into his pocket and handed Karen some medicine Rachel had given him.

Marcus pulled into the driveway as he saw someone peek out the blinds. He made his way up to the front door and knocked. Marcus knocked two more times.

"Eloise, my name is Marcus Slay, may I have a word with you?"

Eloise stood back and listened.

"Eloise, I'm a private investigator. I need to speak with you about the Rodney Jackson trial."

Eloise stood with her hand up to her mouth with a look of fear on her face. Eloise rushed to the phone. She picked up a business card and dialed.

"This is Eloise Johnson, and you told me if anyone came around asking about the trial to call you. Well, someone's here now."

"Hey Mrs. Johnson, don't worry. My men will take care

of things. Did you catch his name?"

"Yes, his name is Marcus Slay. He said he is a private investigator."

Marcus sat for a few minutes before entering the next address into his navigation system.

"Well, I hope I have better luck with Mr. Thompson," Marcus said as he pulled off.

Michael drove up and parked.

Michael looked over at Karen as she slept. She was still holding her side.

"Karen, babe, we're here."

Michael nudged her repeatedly. Finally, Karen awakened.

"Damn, girl. Those pills knocked you out."

Karen said groggily, "Yeah, they did. Where are we?"

"My mom's house."

"You brought me to your mom's house, Michael?"

"Yes, we'll be safe here. No one will think about looking for us here again."

"What do you mean again?"

"It's nothing. Don't worry about it."

Michael got out of the car and went around to the passenger's side. He helped Karen into the house.

Marcus pulled up to Mr. Thompson's home and parked his car. He got out as two men walked out of the home. They made their way to a car that was parked in the driveway. Marcus walked toward them.

"Hello gentlemen, would either of you be Mr. Thompson?"

They both looked Marcus up and down.

"I am, and who are you?"

"I'm Marcus Slay, a private investigator."

The friend of Mr. Thompson, gave an eyebrow raise and a puzzled look as he looked at Mr. Thompson.

"I don't know why you would want to see me?"

"I have a few questions about the Rodney Jackson trial that you were a juror on. I spoke to some other jurors."

"Well, you don't need me."

He started to walk more towards the car.

"Other jurors said they were paid off to vote him guilty, is that true? Were you paid off as well?"

"Man, if I was you, I wouldn't be runnin my trap with this dude, you don't know," Mr. Thompson's friend said.

"I'm legit, you can look me up," Marcus said.

Mr. Thompson said in with a shaky voice, "I'm sure you are, but I can't, we gotta go!"

Mr. Thompson's friend got into the car. Mr. Thompson walked to the passenger side of the car, he waved his friend to hurry and unlock his side.

"Come on, hurry up!"

"Can I leave my card with you? You can remain anonymous." Marcus said.

Mr. Thompson didn't look up, nor did he answer, he just left Marcus standing in his tracks.

I wonder why he and his friend were so nervous?

Marcus got into his car and called Desmond.

"Yeah, man, something ain't right. People are nervous when it comes to this case."

"I would be nervous too, but since they don't want to talk with you, they'll have to talk in court."

"Right, you should have enough evidence now to have the case reopened."

"I know. I'm putting a team together as we speak and I will have the papers drawn up and submitted to the judge to reopen the case."

"Awesome! Just keep me posted. I have one more person I need to speak with and then I will get back to with you.

Karen awakened on the couch.

"Damn, I was out again."

Karen looked down and noticed a clean bandage.

"Michael. Michael! Michael!"

Karen looked around the room in a panic. She saw a note next to a cell phone on the end table beside her. When she opened the paper, it revealed a phone number. She dialed it.

"Hey babe," Michael said.

"Michael? What the fuck? You left me?"

"Babe, I had to. Your accounts are frozen and we need money."

"Oh god, tell me you're not about to do something stupid."

"Of course not... I'm going to rob Stephanie."

"What? Michael, you can't."

"Trust me. I'll just take some jewelry and be in and out. She'll never know it was me. I'm almost there now."

"Are you sure about this?"

"Yes. Just keep the burner beside you and take your meds. Everything's going to be alright. I'mma make sure of it."

"I love you."

"I love you too. Don't worry. I'll be back soon."

"Ok."

Karen hung up and held the phone close. Tears streamed down her face.

"You better be right about this."

Michael parked a few houses down. He snuck around the side. A neighbor's dog barked loudly. Michael hid behind a tree. The neighbor opened his back door and stood on the deck. He swept his yard with a flashlight. He called the dog and they both went inside. The neighbor turned off his outside lights.

Michael maneuvered his way to the back. He opened a window and climbed through it.

Michael closed the window behind him. He glanced around and darted for the hallway. He entered Stephanie's bedroom and located her jewelry box.

"Now, we're talkin."

Michael opened the box.

"What the fuck, Stephanie? Costume jewelry! Really! Where's the real stuff?"

Michael closed the box and continued to search. He checked the nightstand and under the bed. Next, he went into the walk-in closet.

Stephanie opened the garage door and walked in and closed the door. She set the alarm and dialed a number on her cell phone.

Michael found a locked jewelry box. He picked the lock, opened the lid, and pulled out a wedding ring along with other valuables. Michael rejoiced, but then heard a female's voice. The voice grew louder. Michael closed the box and took it with him deeper into the closet.

Stephanie entered the room while on her cell phone.

Michael clutched the box as he watched Stephanie.

Stephanie moved to another side of the room.

"Are you coming by tonight?"

"Yeah, I am heading that way now."

"Ok, cool."

Michael shifted in the closet to get a better view. He knocked over a wig stand but caught it before it fell. He tried to see if Stephanie had left, but couldn't get a good view. He listened and didn't hear her voice.

Stephanie struggled at her dresser as she tried to take off a stubborn earring. She rounded the corner toward her closet just as Michael stepped out of the closet with the jewelry box. Michael and Stephanie came face-to-face.

Stephanie stood in shock, "Michael?"

Michael didn't move. Stephanie saw the jewelry box in Michael's hands and her eyes grew big.

"Oh my God, what are you doing?"

Michael tried to go around Stephanie, but Stephanie reached for the box. Michael moved it out of her reach, he tried to leave, but Stephanie got in his way.

"Move, Stephanie," Michael said.

"No! Not until you give me my stuff back."

"Don't make me do this the hard way."

"And don't make me call the cops on you!"

Stephanie again reached for the box. This time she got a hand on it. Michael and Stephanie wrestled with the box of jewelry.

"Let go, Bitch!"

"No! You can't have it!"

The box slipped and fell to the floor. Some of the jewelry spilled out. Stephanie dived onto the floor and Michael dived right after her. She clutched her wedding ring. Michael punched Stephanie hard in the face with his fist. She lay on the floor out cold.

Michael shook his head, "Damn, Bitch. Why do you always have to do things the hard way? There was a time when I used to like you, too. Shit!"

Michael hastily picked up the jewelry and ran out the door. Stephanie lay lifeless as the security alarm Michael triggered blared through the house.

Jason arrived slightly ahead of the police. He heard the alarm and saw sirens as they approached in the near distance. Jason rushed inside.

"Stephanie! Steph! Can you hear me, baby?"

Jason ran from room to room calling out to her.

Jason stopped at the door. He saw Stephanie as she lay unconscious on the floor.

"Oh, Steph! Who did this to you?"

Jason fell to his knees and hugged her.

"C'mon, baby. Please wake up."

He felt a pulse and heard the sirens that had arrived. He picked her up, and as he turned to the door, her hand opened, and the ring fell to the ground and swiveled. The police burst into the room.

"Freeze!"

The next morning, Marcus pulled into the parking lot. He was on the phone when he noticed two Hispanic men approach him.

"Yo, you Marcus Slay?" The first man asked

"Yeah, who wants to know? Hold on, babe."

The second man pulled out a gun and held it to Marcus's head.

"This is a warning to you, leave the Rodney Jackson case alone, if not, that pretty little wife of yours..."

Marcus cut him off.

"You better keep my wife out of this!"

"Like I was saying, leave the case alone, it's a done deal!" The first man said.

The man with the gun hit Marcus in the head with the butt of the gun. Marcus fell to the ground.

Mrs. Slay heard the men, and all at once, she heard the phone drop.

"Marcus! Marcus, what's going on?" Mrs. Slay yelled.

Mrs. Slay was still on the phone as she rushed out of the house.

Mrs. Slays pulled into the parking lot thirty minutes later to find several police cars and the paramedics.

CHAPTER 16

They kept Stephanie overnight at the hospital. The next day she sat on the bed dressed when Jason walked in. He walked over and kissed her on the lips.

"Hey, how are you feeling?"

"My head hurts a little, but other than that, I am fine."

"Are you ready to go?"

"Yes, but I am not sure how I feel about going home."

"Don't worry, I will be there, and besides, Michael is not that stupid to come back this time."

"I don't know. This is the second time he's been there."

"How did he get in without the alarm system detecting him?"

"I was thinking about that. He must've already been in the house when I set it."

Michael walked inside his mom's house and saw Karen on the couch asleep. He walked over and shook her. Karen opened her eyes and smiled.

"Hey, is everything okay? Did you get the jewelry from Stephanie?"

Michael held up the cash in his hand.

"Yes I did and I have already pawned it."

"Is that all you got?"

"Yeah."

"How's my baby feeling?"

"The medicine knocked out a lot of the pain, but it also knocks me out. Babe, I'm worried, I don't want to go back to jail."

"The only thing you need to worry about right now, is getting better."

"And then what? What are we going to do? We need to leave the country or something."

"That sounds nice, but where are we going to get the money for that."

"We have to think of something, maybe you can rob a bank."

Michael laughed loudly, "Right, do you think I'm crazy?"

"Pretty much. When I get better, we can do it together. But we have to have a solid plan so we don't get caught."

"You're serious, aren't you?"

"Dead serious. That's the only way we are going to survive."

Jason and Stephanie made their way inside.

"Man, that breakfast was so good. I'm ready for a nap now." Stephanie said as she took her shoes off.

"That's fine. I have the day off so I will be here while you sleep."

Stephanie moved further inside when she saw her wedding ring. She bent down to pick it up. She held the ring up in her hand.

"This is what he really wanted, but I was not going to depart with this."

"Was that ring that important?"

"Yes, it's my wedding rin..."

Jason eyed Stephanie.

"Oh, I see, the ring that Desmond gave you."

"Why do you have to say it like that?"

Jason shook his head.

"Go ahead and take your nap. I will be here when you awake."

Jason made himself comfortable on the couch.

Desmond sat at his desk. He pulled out his cell phone and dialed.

"Marcus! Man, where have you been? I have been trying to reach you."

"My fault. I have been meaning to call you. I was jumped by two men."

"What! Are you ok?"

"Yeah, but they got me good."

"Was it about the case?"

"Yeah, one said before busting me upside the head to leave the Rodney Jackson case alone."

"Damn, man! I'm sorry I got you into this. Things are getting crazy," Desmond said.

"Well, I'm glad you called because I need to show you something."

"Bro, this ain't worth no one getting hurt over. Let's just evaluate this later, " Desmond said.

"Naw, they bust me in my fucking head. This just makes me want to dig more into this case. Anyway, I have something you're going to want to see," Marcus said.

"Ok, see you soon."

Desmond sat the phone down on the desk and opened his laptop when he heard a knock at the door. The door opened.

"You busy?" Candice asked.

Desmond looked up and was surprised to see Candice.

"To what, do I owe this spontaneous visit?"

Candice pushed the door closed, turn the lock, set her purse on the desk, and walk behind Desmond where he sat in his chair.

"Well, I wanted to apologize for how I acted the other morning."

"You didn't have to come all the way down here to apologize."

Candice said seductively, "True, but I forgot how much fun

129

we use to have in this office."

Desmond smiled, "We did have some great times."

Candice ran her hands down Desmond chest and spun him around to face her. Candice kneeled down and unzipped Desmond's pants.

"I'm sorry!" Candice said.

Desmond's head tilted back as he moaned. Once he released himself, Candice stood up, walked around to the front of the desk, picked up her purse that fell to the floor, and walked to the door and unlocked it.

"So, am I forgiven for the way my mother treated you?" Candice turned around.

"I didn't say that," Candice said.

"So, what was that, that just happen?"

"Nothing! I just felt like sucking your dick. Did you like it?"

"Huh, I think you know the answer to that."

"Good, I'll see you at home."

Candice walked out. Desmond sat with a smile on his face. He stood up and fixed his clothes and out of the corner of his eye, Desmond saw something on the floor. He picked it up and looked at it.

Desmond was confused, "A toll receipt," He said.

Later that afternoon, Desmond and Marcus sat around the conference room table.

"Check this out."

Marcus slid a folder over to Desmond.

"This is definitely enough evidence for a retrial, but there's one little problem."

"What's that?"

"That judge. If he was in on it, then he is not going to grant me a new trial."

"Is there any way around it?"

130

"I don't know. My team is checking into that now."
Desmond gave a big sigh and leaned back in the chair.

"Ok. Is everything ok?"

"I don't know, I can't quite put my finger on it."

"Anything, I can help with?"

"Man, you've done enough already. I don't want to put anything more on your plate."

"What is it?"
Desmond stood up, went into his pocket, pulled out the receipt, and handed it to Marcus.

"It's a toll receipt."

"Yeah, it fell out my wife's purse. I want to know where she was and when."
Marcus looked confused, "Ok."

"You think you can look into it?"

"Yeah, sure. I'll let you know what I find out."
Desmond sat behind his desk with his hands locked behind his head when he heard a knock at the door.

"Come in," Desmond said.
Todd Ransom walked through the door.

"Tell me you got some good news."
Todd took a seat in front of Desmond's desk.

"I'm afraid not. You're going to have to go through Judge Randall for the retrial."

"Damn! Are you sure there's no other way around it?"

"I'm Positive. I'll have my paralegal send the request. Now all we got to do is sit back and wait."

"Yeah, and in the mean time, I will do some more research of my own. I appreciate your help though."

Michael and Karen pulled into a parking space. A few customers exited the building.

"This is the perfect time of day to hit this bank. Most of

131

the customers have left." Michael said.

"I still can't believe you really want to do this."

"Just stick to the plan. We'll be fine."

"Okay, whatever you say. I'll scope it out."

Michael got out of the car and went inside the bank. Karen turned up the radio. She surveyed the foot traffic around the bank. She also looked for outside cameras.

Michael entered and tried to blend in. He pulled his baseball cap down to his eyes. He walked over to the counter and grabbed a slip and a pen. There were only a hand full of customers.

Michael counted two cameras and noticed that there was one security guard. The tellers quickly cleared the short line. Brian came up behind Michael.

"Hello, I'm Brian, the assistant bank manager. Is there anything I can help you with, sir?"

"Huh, oh no. I'm just. I was. I need to make a withdrawal, but I forgot my account number."

"That's ok, sir. We are happy to look that up for you."

"No, no I don't want to take up your time."

"It's no trouble at all, but I do need to ask you to please remove your hat."

"It's ok. My wife is in the car. We're running late, so I'll just come back some other time."

Michael rushed to the exit. Brian followed him to the door. Michael hopped inside and startled Karen. He put the car in gear and took off.

"Well, what happened?"

"Reality check. That's what."

"Huh? What are you talking about, Michael?"

"I should have known better than to think a black man could just walk into a bank without getting questioned."

"That's ridiculous."

Karen crossed her arms and shook her head in disbelief.

"I bet he won't be so smug when we take all their money. I'm going to make Brian beg for mercy. Let's do this."

"Brian? Ok, whatever. I don't want to hurt anybody."
Michael pulled over.

"You didn't see the way he looked at me. Like I couldn't possibly have an account there."

"Well, you don't."

"He ain't know that. He just assumed. You don't know what that's like, Karen."

"Sorry, babe. I can't stand people like that. We're gonna make him beg."

"Yeah."

Stephanie was sleeping when she started having a nightmare about the attack.

Stephanie screamed, "No! Get off me! Get off me!"

Jason ran into the room and shook Stephanie out of her sleep.

"Stephanie, wake up!"

Stephanie awakened in tears. She saw Jason and hugged him tight.

Stephanie began to weep, "Oh, Jason. I can't get him out of my head!"

"It's ok, Steph. I'm here. We'll get through this."

Stephanie made room for Jason beside her on the bed.

"Will you lay with me?"

"Of course."

Jason got in and put his arm around Stephanie. She snuggled up against his chest, closed her eyes, and exhaled.

"I feel so much better when you're around."

Stephanie opened her eyes and looked up at Jason. He held

her tighter. Their eyes locked, and they moved in for a tender kiss.

"As long as I'm around, I won't let nothing happen to you."

Stephanie put her hand on Jason's face. She pulled him in for another kiss. She wrapped her leg in between his and rested her hand on his manhood. Jason unbuttoned Stephanie's pajama top as they continued to kiss. Stephanie sat up to pull her arms out of the top and revealed her naked breast. Jason took a moment to embrace this vision.

"You're so beautiful."

Stephanie smiled. Jason sat up, kissed her neck and cuffed her breast. Stephanie rubbed his head and pulled his shirt off over his head.

"Are you sure this is what you want?"

"Very sure."

Jason pulled down his pants and let the dragon out of his cage. He lifted Stephanie on top of him, and the two embraced. Stephanie moaned as she wrapped her legs around Jason's back. They interlocked fingers and licked all over as they glided back and forth.

Jason rolled Stephanie onto her stomach doggy style, and they reached a beautiful climax.

The next day, Stephanie was at Jason's home for dinner.

"I'm very impressed, that was a very tasty meal."

"I know my way around the kitchen enough to pull off a little magic."

"That you did," Stephanie said as she gave Jason a flirtatious smile and leaned over to kiss Jason.

"Hold on, I have something else for you."

Jason went into the kitchen and brought back a bowl of ice cream.

"One bowl?" Stephanie asked as she was surprised.

"Yes. You'll see why in a minute."
Jason fed Stephanie the ice cream and it dripped on her lip.

"That's mine. I get my ice cream every time it lands on your pretty lips, or elsewhere."
Stephanie giggled as Jason kissed her lips. Jason continued to feed her the ice cream and Stephanie let it fall to her chest. Jason leaned down and licked it off. He caressed Stephanie's breasts with a stroke of his tongue. She moaned. Stephanie reached for Jason's body and pulled him closer to her.

"You know I want you, but first follow me," Jason said as he led her to his master bathroom and turned the shower on.

"Allow me to undress you."
Stephanie nodded her head in agreement.

"Ok."
Jason removed each piece of Stephanie's garments. He looked at her body as Stephanie started to undress him. They stepped into the shower and lathered each other until he could no longer resist. Jason slipped his dragon between Stephanie's thighs from behind, but he didn't enter her. He lets his dragon slide in the suds close to her treasure and after the tease he finally gave her what they both wanted. He inserted himself inside of her and with long, deep, gentle strokes, he held her close as they climaxed together. The water, rinsed the suds and the evidence of their lovemaking away.

"Let me get you a towel," Jason said.
He grabbed the towel and looked into her eyes.

"Steph, will you stay the night?"

"Yes, I'd like that, but you better get ready for round two."

135

"Girl I'm a personal trainer, and Mr. 2020, so I stay ready."
They both laughed. Ha-ha.

CHAPTER 17

Michael looked at Karen.

Karen said nervously, "Are you sure we can do this?"

"Baby, look! We have cased this bank for weeks. We're ready. You remember the plan?"

"Yes, I remember."

"Ok, then let's do the damn thing."

"Ok."

Karen reached for the door handle. Michael grabbed Karen's arm.

"Hey, I love you!"

"I love you too."

Karen leaned over and kissed Michael.

"No matter what happens, we're in this together," Michael said.

Karen and Michael exited the car. They entered the bank. Michael walked over to the table while Karen stood in line.

"Next in line," The teller said.

Karen walked up towards the counter.

The teller smiled. "How may I help you?"

Karen looked over at Michael, who walked up to the security officer.

"Excuse me, can you tell me..."

Brian walked up.

"Hey, I remember you. You're back. Are you wanting to open an account with us?"

Michael looked over at Karen and gave her a nod.

Karen leaned forward and pointed a gun at the teller.

"I need you to put all the money in these bags," Karen whispered.

Karen sat the bags on the counter.

"I'm sorry, but I..." The teller was scared.
Michael quickly grabbed the gun off the Security Officer's waist and pointed at Brian.

"Naw, I'm making a withdrawal. Now get yo racist ass on the floor!"

"Bitch, put it all in there!" Karen shouted.
Michael looked down at Brian.

"I'm sorry. I don't want any trouble. Please don't shoot me. I have a family," Brian pleaded.
Karen laughed.

"You're a racist piece of shit. You harass people of color and make them feel less than you. I should shoot you."

"No, please!"
The teller pressed the silent alarm under the counter. Karen looked back at the teller.

"Bitch, did you press that button?" Karen yelled.

"Yes," The teller cried.
Michael panicked. "Oh shit! We got to go, babe get the money, and let's go!"
The teller sat the bag on the counter. Karen grabbed the bags and gave a bag to Michael. Brian begged for his life.

"I'm sorry."

"You're lucky I ain't got time today."

"Come on!" Michael yelled.
Michael ran out the door. Karen looked down and saw the bag half full.

"We need more money," Karen said.
Karen went back to the counter.
Meanwhile, Michael started the engine.

"What is she doing," Michael said as he became more nervous.

Michael looked through the rearview mirror. He saw and heard the police sirens.

"Didn't, I say fill it up! Don't make me use this, bitch," Karen stood there arguing with the teller.

Karen tossed the bag over the counter. She heard the police sirens and looked back at the door. She snatched the bag off the counter and ran to the door.

The police pulled up, jumped out of their cars, and drew their guns.

"Come out with your hands up!"

Karen dropped the bag and raised her hands in the air.

Stephanie had awakened just as Jason walked into the bedroom with a tray with breakfast and coffee.

Stephanie wiped her eyes and sat up in bed.

"My God! This smells delicious. Are you going to join me?"

Jason stood at the window. He wanted to slap himself.

"No, I'm not really hungry."

"Are you okay? It seems as if something is bothering you."

"I broke my rule."

"Your rule," Stephanie said.

"Yes, my rule to never let a woman spend the night with me, and I have broken it twice."

Stephanie stopped eating and looked at Jason.

"Let me guess, Marsha was the first person?"

Jason shook his head yes, but never turned around.

"Okay, I see."

Stephanie stopped eating and got out of bed, and with tears in her eyes, she reached for her clothes. Jason stood at the window until he heard the front door shut. Jason was heartbroken. He loved Stephanie more than he cared to, and now he doesn't know how to handle it. Jason continued to

think about how he felt when his wife broke his heart. He
was afraid that Stephanie would do the same. This was the
reason Jason continued to deal with Marsha. He knew he
could never fall in love with her. Marsha was safe.
Later that evening, Stephanie sat on the couch in tears as
she continued to call Jason.

"Come on Jason, call me back. I know you're not that
busy!"
There was a knock at the door. Stephanie looked up and
yelled loudly in frustration, "Who is it!"
Minutes later, Sophia walked in. She stopped when she saw
her sister.

"Hey, sis."
Stephanie sighed and rolled her eyes.

"Now, is that any way to treat your sister?"
Sophia moved further into the home.

"I'm not in the mood for company."

"I'm not company, I'm your family. I know I haven't
been a good sister, but now I want to make up for it."
Sophia walked over to Stephanie and stopped.

"Steph, what's wrong?"

"I'm sure you want to hear so you can say, I knew it."

"That would be the old me. I need to tell you what
happened to Nick and me, and that I lost the baby."

Jason rolled off of Marsha. Jason lets out a deep breath
as Marsha continued to lay on her stomach. She reached for
Jason, but he jumped out of bed and put his pants on.
Marsha picked up her robe from the floor and went to the
bathroom. Jason pulled his phone out of his pocket. He saw
Stephanie's phone calls.

"You know you can stay."

"I know, but that's ok. I got work to do at the gym."
Jason stared at the picture of Stephanie on his phone.

140

"Seriously?" Marsha said as she flushed the toilet.

"Can't we just spend a day together?

Jason put the phone back in his pocket and grabbed his shoes.

"I'm sorry. Maybe next time. I really do have to go."

Marsha reentered the room with a towel to wipe her hands. Jason sat on the bed. Marsha sat next to him. She took his hand and rubbed it between her legs.

"You feel that? Doesn't it feel better than working?"

Jason rubbed her for a minute, and then he moved his hand away. He put on his shoes.

"It does, but if I keep messing with you, I'll go bankrupt."

Jason got up to leave.

"Aww, so you gonna leave me just like that."

Marsha opened her robe and lay back. Jason turned around and looked at her.

Jason smiled. "Yep."

Jason walked out. Marsha smiled to herself.

Marsha said quietly, "That's what you think. I'm gonna make you forget all about that bitch, Stephanie."

"I'm so sorry to hear you lost the baby, I didn't know! I would've reached out."

Stephanie hugged Sophia, and they embraced for a few seconds.

"I know you would've. It's ok, I was so broken when it happened, I couldn't wrap my head around it."

"Does mom and dad know?"

"Yes, they do, and I asked them to let me tell you."

"Would you like a cup of coffee?"

"Sure."

Stephanie got up and walked into the kitchen.

141

Stephanie poured herself and Sophia a cup of coffee and sat back down.

"I don't feel like eating, but if you want something to eat, I can prepare you something."

Sophia shook her head.

"No, I'm good. I want to say I'm sorry for how I acted in the past, and I want you to know I've grown from this."

"What do you mean?"

Sophia moved closer to Stephanie and touched her hand.

"I don't jump to conclusions anymore, and I hear people out. I apologize for not giving you that respect and empathy in the past."

"That's all I wanted more than anything. I wanted to know that my sister had my back."

Sophia sat back and stared off.

"I didn't even see it coming."

"See what?"

"Nick and his lover. He jogs in Sahm park every evening."

Sophia looked at Stephanie.

"I went to surprise him with a bottle of Gatorade, and I got surprised when I saw him and his lover."

"What did you see?"

"Them, hot and heavy in his SUV."

"Well, did you know her?"

"No, and it wasn't a her it was a he. I was so stressed out about it, I lost the baby. Enough about that. Why do you keep checking your phone?"

"Wow," Stephanie said in shock.

"Well, Jason and I have become more than friends, and now he's ignoring my phone calls."

Michael paced back and forth.

"Damn! I can't believe she got caught."

Michael walked over to the couch. He opened the bags of money and started to count.

Michael lay the money across the coffee table. He stared at the money and ran his hand over his hair.

"A half a mill. Damn, I could triple that in no time. Hollywood casino, look out because here I come!"

Michael gathered the money and placed it back into one big black duffle bag. He left out en route to the casino.

Jason sat behind his desk with his fingers locked behind his head as he leaned back.

He thought back to the time when he was at Stephanie's.

They stepped into the shower and lathered each other until he could no longer resist. Jason slipped his dragon between Stephanie's thighs from behind.

A knock at the door interrupted Jason's thoughts.

Jason leaned forward in his chair.

"Come in."

Marsha walked through the door.

"What are you doing here?"

"I came by to see if you would like to join me for a drink?"

Jason rubbed his hand across his face.

"Or we could go over to BDubs to watch the game, eat, and have a couple of beers."

Jason thought about it for a minute.

"That does sound good. Give me about thirty minutes, and I will meet you over there."

Desmond sat at his desk as he read a letter. He frowned and looked out his door and saw his secretary at her desk.

"Cynthia, can you step into my office?" He yelled out to her.

Cynthia grabbed her notepad, got up, and stepped inside his office.

"Yes, sir."

"Contact Judge Randall's secretary and set up a meeting with him for today, not tomorrow or next week, but today!" Desmond got up and paced the floor.

"This is regarding Rodney Jackson's retrial."

"I'll do my best."

"And relay this message. If I don't get an appointment, I'll make my own."

An hour later, Desmond sat in the Judge's office.

"I got your urgent message, and I want to say I don't understand what you plan on accomplishing."

"A retrial for my client that he lawfully deserves."

"How so? He was found guilty in the court of law."

"Was he? It was more like his rights were overlooked along with the lack of evidence."

"What's your point in all this? There's no reason to waste the taxpayer's money with this non-sense."

"I beg to differ, and I'm sure the media would love to know you were paid off in the first trial."

Desmond pressed the button on his phone and hit the speaker button.

"Fox 59, how may I help you."

"Ok! Ok!."

Desmond hung up.

"Don't press your luck, and you better watch yourself." Judge Randall said.

Judge Randall stood up, and so did Desmond.

"How soon will my client get a retrial?"

"The court will contact your office."

"Oh, and one more thing, I want a new judge for the trial."

CHAPTER 18

"**W**elcome to AMC. What can I get for you?"
The cashier asked.

"I'd like a large bucket of popcorn and a drink."

"That'll be $17.96."

Stephanie paid. She took her popcorn and cup over to the drink machine to fill up. A couple walked by and laughed loudly.

Marsha laughed. "Oh, Jason."

Stephanie stopped and turned her head toward the sound. She saw Marsha wrap her arm around Jason's arm as they walked past her.

"Oh, I am so excited about the trial today."

"Why? I can see Trina being excited, but why are you excited?"

"I'm happy for her. Trina's man, maybe coming home."

Desmond stared at Candice. He got up from the table, walked over and kissed her, and walked out of the house.

Rodney sat with his two attorneys. He looked around the court room for Candice when he heard the bailiff.

"Please rise. The court of the second Judicial Circuit Criminal Division is now in session, the Honorable Judge Sara Stevenson presiding."

Sara Stevenson walked in exuding confidence. She scanned the room before sitting.

"Everyone but the jury may be seated. Mr. Reynolds, please swear in the jury."

The bailiff walked over to the jury pool.

"Please raise your right hand. Do you solemnly swear or affirm that you will truly listen to this case and render a true verdict and a fair sentence as to this defendant?"

"I do," The jury said in unison.

"You may be seated."

"Mr. Reynolds, what is today's case?"

"Your Honor, today's case is the retrial for Rodney Jackson, versus the state of Indiana."

"Is the prosecuting attorney and defense attorney's ready?"

"Yes, your honor," The prosecuting attorney said.

"Yes, your honor,' The defense attorney's said.

"Mr. Hensley, please call your first witness."

"Your honor, I would like to call Trey Jones to the stand."

Everyone turned to look as Trey approached the stand. Trey was sworn in and Mr. Hensley approached Trey.

"Trey Jones, on the night of March 19, 2019. Tell us what happened between Rodney Jackson and James Taylor. And remember you are under oath."

"On the night of March 19, my friend Rodney Jackson was at my club. I witnessed him and James Taylor arguing, and minutes later, James walked out the door, and Rodney followed."

Mr. Hensley walked over and grabbed his notes from the desk.

"Let me read your testimony from September 9, 2019. You said in your own words that Rodney Jackson had it in for James Taylor and that he was the one that shot him outside your club. Did you not say that Mr. Jones?'

"No, I did not say that! The prosecuting attorney came to my club and I showed him the footage from that night and that was it."

"So what you are saying is that you never signed this affidavit?"

Mr. Hensley walked over to Trey and handed him the affidavit.

"No, I did not, and that is not my signature."

"So what you're saying is someone forged your signature?"

"Yes, if you're saying I signed this form here."

"No more questions your honor."

Mr. Taylor, would you like to cross-examine the witness?

"No, your honor. But I would like to call to the stand Mrs. Lorraine Johnson."

Candice paced back and forth.

"Damn! I wish I could be there."

Candice grabbed her purse, keys, and headed out.

Lorraine took the stand and was sworn in.

"Mrs. Johnson, can you tell us what happened while being in the jury pool for the trial of Rodney Jackson."

After being sworn in she stated, "Well, we all voted in the jury room to vote not guilty, but the next day four of the jurors came back and told us to vote guilty. They bullied us into voting their way."

"So what you are telling us is that you guys did not believe Mr. Jackson was guilty of the crime he was accused of."

"Objection, your honor. He's putting words in the witness's mouth," Mr. Hensley said.

"Overruled," The judge said. "You may continue, Mrs. Johnson."

"Not at all. There was no evidence to prove otherwise. There was talk about the four jurors being paid to vote the other way and to convince us to do so."

"I object your honor. That's here say."

"Objection overruled. Continue Mrs. Johnson," The judge said.

"Can you explain to us what happened on the day you guys came up with the verdict?" Desmond asked.

"Right before we voted, we got a visit from two men and the judge. The two men told us it would be in our best interest to vote guilty."

"And how did you feel about that?"

Lorraine looked around the courtroom, "I was scared so I voted guilty, but now I know that wasn't right, so I'm here to make my wrong, right."

Desmond turned to look at the judge and shook his head.

"That will be all, your honor."

"Mr. Hensley, would you like to cross-examine the witness?"

"Yes, I would."

Mr. Hensley walked over to the stand.

"Remember, you are under oath. Now what you are saying is that some jurors, two unknown men, and the judge convinced you guys to vote Rodney Jackson guilty?"

"Yes, the judge, the men, and four of the jurors convinced us."

"So when you were sworn into the jury pool, you swore to render a true verdict and a fair sentence to the defendant. But you didn't do that, so now how are we supposed to believe what you're telling us today is true. You've lied under oath before?"

"Objection, your Honor. The witness clearly stated that she felt threatened," Desmond yelled.

"Sustained!" The judge said.

"No more questions, your honor."

"Mr. Taylor, would you like to call your second witness."

"No, but I would like to approach the bench, your honor."

148

Desmond approached the bench and so did Mr. Hensley.

"Your honor, I would like the jurors to see the evidence that convicted Rodney Jackson."

The judge nodded and Mr. Hensley walked back to his desk as Desmond walked over and stood in front of the jury pool.

"I want you guys to see what evidence convicted my client. And then, I hope you guys come with an honest verdict."

The jurors watched the screen as it showed Rodney and a woman arguing. Desmond leaned in further as he looked at the female Rodney was arguing with and looked back at Marcus. The jurors saw Rodney arguing with a man. The man left out and about two minutes later, Rodney walked out the door.

Desmond got up and approached the jurors. He addressed the jurors.

"You saw my client, arguing with a female and then a man. He didn't murder the woman so why was he convicted of murdering the man. There is no evidence to prove he committed the crime. My client has been framed.

Desmond walked back to his seat.

"We will convene in two hours with a verdict."

Desmond stood outside the courthouse with his team. Desmond looked at his watch.

"Hey, guys, we should head back inside."

The group walked toward the door when Desmond saw Candice as she walked up.

"You guys go ahead. I'll meet you inside."

Candice walked up to Desmond.

Todd eyed Candice and shook his head before going inside.

"Hey, what are you doing here?" Desmond asked.

"I was on pins and needles in the house and I could not

149

wait any longer to hear the verdict, so I'm here."

"Is Trina here?"

"How would I know?"

Desmond and Candice walked into the courtroom together. Candice took a seat far in the back on the right-hand side so she could get a good look at Rodney, while Desmond took his seat up front with his team.

"After hearing the case of Rodney Jackson versus the state of Indiana. It saddens me to think that in 2020, a black man still can't get a fair trial, and with that being said, I will read the verdict."

The bailiff passed the judge the votes. Rodney and his team stood as the verdict was read.

"We the jury find the defendant, Rodney Jackson, not guilty in the murder of James Taylor."

Rodney turned around with the biggest smile on his face and scanned the room when his eyes met Candice. He stared directly at her. Desmond turned to see Rodney and saw him as he stared at Candice.

Karen walked in. The inmates began to whisper to each other. Karen grabbed a tray and stood in line.

Susan looked over at Karen as she took a bite of her toast.

"I guess this bitch thought she was Wonder Woman."

The inmates at the table laughed.

Susan smiled, "Well the bitch couldn't have been too smart."

Karen slowly walked past Susan and sat at the table. Another inmate sat at the table with Karen.

"Man, I thought I wasn't going to ever see you again. But then I saw you on the news."

"Can you get me a phone? I need to get in touch with somebody."

"Yeah, for sure."

"Alright, ladies chow time is up, line up!" The correctional officer said.

The inmates stood in line. Susan and her girls walked past Karen. Susan stopped next to Karen and leaned over and whispered, "You heal fast. Welcome back."

The correctional officer yelled, "Move it!"

Three weeks later, Karen and Susan's trial had begun.

The Judge walked in.

"All rise!" The bailiff said.

Karen, Susan, and their lawyers stood. The judge sat down.

"You may be seated." The bailiff said.

"We are here for the sentencing of Susan Smith and Karen Jamison for embezzlement. Will the defendants please stand.

Karen, Susan and their lawyers stood.

"Ms. Smith and Ms. Jamison You have been charged with embezzlement and have been found guilty in a court of law. Ms. Smith, you will serve a term of ten years with the possibility of parole after serving five consecutive years. Ms. Jamison, you will also serve a term of ten years plus an additional five years for your escape totaling fifteen years to be served without the possibility of parole. The court is adjourned!" The Bailiff's escorted Susan and Karen out of the courtroom.

On the way to the casino, Michael's saw a sign advertising for an open house coming up for a home for sale.

Why am I going to the casino?

He rode by the house instead to look at it.

This is what I need. My spot nice and secluded.

Desmond walked into the bedroom to find Candice at the dresser as she applied her lipstick. He walked further inside, stood in the back of her, and wrapped his arms around her waist.

"What's the occasion?" Desmond asked.

Candice turned to face Desmond.

"Trina is throwing Rodney a release party."

Desmond pulled Candice to him.

"And I'm not invited? The man who pulled this all off. You and I both know Rodney was guilty as hell," Desmond said sarcastically.

Desmond tried to kiss Candice, but she pulled away.

Irritated Candice said, "Don't you mess up my lipstick!"

Desmond backed away and looked at her sideways. Candice blew him a kiss, grabbed her purse, and headed out of the bedroom. She yelled over her shoulder.

"Don't wait up for me."

Desmond shook his head.

"Ain't that a bitch!" Desmond said.

Candice pulled into the driveway, Rodney stood at the door and they ran to meet each other.

Candice was so excited, "Oh my God! Babe, I can't believe you are really home!"

Candice touched Rodney's face. She stood on her tiptoes and pulled his face down to meet hers.

Rodney picked Candice up and swung her around as they locked lips with each other.

Trina walked to the door and saw Rodney and Candice.

Trina yelled, "Damn! Get a room!"

"Naw, you get a room!" Rodney yelled back.

"Don't worry, I'm getting out of y'all hair. My man is on his way now."

Later that evening after Trina had left, Rodney prepared dinner for the two of them.

"You want the main course first or the dessert?"

"It all depends on what's for dessert?"

Rodney grabbed his dick.

"This is for dessert."

"I always like a little dessert before the main course," Candice said seductively.

CHAPTER 19

Michael drove to the back door in the alley of the pool hall.

Michael looked around and approached the door, and knocked.

An old handyman opened the door. "Whatcha looking for?"

"I need a new social card and birth certificate."

The handyman was skeptical. "You got money?"

"Yes, I do, and if you can do this for me, I can give you a little something extra."

"Well, come on in here, boy!"

Michael walked in and looked around. "You got the equipment in here?"

"Naw, come on back here."

Michael walked into another room.

"Have a seat right here and look into the camera."

Michael looked up and faced the camera, and after a few seconds, the handyman led Michael back to the other room to the table.

"You got the money?"

"Right here, and like I promised, I have something extra for you."

Michael passed the handyman an envelope. The handyman looked inside it and put it aside.

"Here are your new driver's license and birth certificate."

The handyman pushed the documents over to Michael to view.

"I must say, your work is good! You definitely live up to your name."

"Right, right you need it, I got it."

"Thanks, man."

"Sign right here, and we will be out of your way," The delivery man said.

Michael signed the furniture delivery ticket and watched as the delivery men got into the truck and left. He sat down.

Karen, I wish you were here baby. I bought this house for us and you're not even here.

Desmond lay on the couch as he watched TV when his phone rang.

"You good?" Marcus asked.

"Yeah, why wouldn't I be?"

"I just got a phone call, and it wasn't a pleasant one."

"From who?"

"The guys I had a run-in with about Rodney's case, and they mentioned your name. They're coming after us."

"What!" Desmond said nervously.

"I called into my contact at the police department, and she ran this by her boss, so if you see an unmarked car, it's IMPD.

Rodney lay on his back as Candice made her way down his body. She came to a stop when she reached his pipe.

"I forgot how big you were."

Rodney enjoyed the feel of Candice's lips wrapped around him.

"Shit, this feels so damn good! You always knew how to work that mouth."

The next morning, Desmond walked out the door as Candice pulled into the driveway. Desmond stood and watched as she got out of the car. She switched past him.

Candice smiled "Good morning, sunshine."

Desmond turned to look at her.

"Excuse me. Can you tell me why you are just now getting home?"

"Oh, I'm sorry. I started to call you last night, but I didn't want to wake you. I had too much to drink, so I spent the night at Trina's."

"Are you serious? When I get home, we need to have a serious talk!" Desmond was fuming."

Later that day, Stephanie was sitting on the couch when the doorbell rang. Stephanie got up from the couch and opened the front door.

"I got here as quick as I can. What's going on?" Sophia asked.

"I need you to go somewhere with me."

"Where are we going?"

"Over to Jason's."

"Are you sure?"

"Yes, I want him to tell me to my face."

"Ok, let's do it!"

Stephanie and Sophia walked out of the house.

Twenty minutes later, Stephanie pulled up in front of Jason's home and parked.

"Are you sure this is a good idea?"

Stephanie sighed. "No, but he owes me the respect to tell me to my face."

"Ok, but if his ass get out of pocket, just know we got you."

"We?"

Sophia went into her purse and pulled out her gun.

"Yes, we."

Stephanie smiled.

"Girl put that away!"

"I'm just saying."

Stephanie opened the door and got out.

Stephanie stood for a moment, then knocked. Jason quickly opened the door.

"About time, I was star... Stephanie!" Jason was surprised.

"Wrong bitch! I guess you were expecting her, huh?"

"Um... I."

Stephanie cut him off.

"That's ok, you don't have to answer that. Look, the only reason I came here is for you to be a man and tell me to my face."

A car pulled up in the driveway. Marsha got out of the car with a bag and began to walk to the front door.

Sophia looked over to see Marsha. Sophia grabbed her purse and opened the door.

"Aw hell Naw, it ain't gonna be that type of party tonight."

Jason, Stephanie, and Marsha turned to see Sophia run across the street and toward them.

Jason whispered, "Stephanie, I'm sorry!"

"You damn right about that," Stephanie yelled.

Marsha walked up to Jason and looked at Stephanie.

"Hey babe, I got that orange chicken you love. What's she doing here?"

"Girl, boo!"

"Marsha not now!" Jason said.

"I know she ain't begging to get you back."

"Bitch, I don't beg."

"Well, all them text and calls say different."

Stephanie looked over at Jason with disgust.

"I can't believe you. I thought better of you, Jason. Have a nice life."

Stephanie turned and walked away.

"Oh, we plan on it, all three of us."

Stephanie stopped, but didn't turn around, tears rolled down her face. Jason looked at Marsha in shock. Marsha went inside while Jason stood on the porch and watched Stephanie pull off. His heart broke in half. He wanted her so bad, but his fear of being hurt again kept him away from her.

Desmond sat on the couch talking to Marcus on the phone.

"Did you find any information on Candice?"

"I searched her name, and with it being so common it came up several times and one hit said she committed suicide. I'm still digging because the suicide name lead had some activity after the death."

"Okay, let me know what you find out."

"It may be nothing, but I thought it was strange how she and Rodney were looking at each other in court."

"Yeah, I thought she was happy for her cousin, but now I don't know what to think."

"Well, you looked as shocked as I was at how Rodney was staring straight at her smiling after the verdict was read."

"Right, I was, but I blew it off at the time since his girl wasn't there. I figured he locked on to someone he knew."

"I got a gut feeling something's off."

"Right, they had a release party for him and didn't invite me. Then she didn't come home that night."

"Another red flag," Marcus said.

"I need you to check Rodney's girlfriend Trina out too. Start with her address. I'm sending it to you now."

"I'll get on it."

"Did you find out anything about the receipt I gave you? I don't know what Candice was doing in Terra Haute."

"Not yet, I'm waiting on the camera surveillance to see

if she was alone or not. Don't worry, I won't leave no stone unturned."

Marsha set the food bag on the counter. Jason followed her.

"What was that?" Jason asked.

"What was what?"

Marsha took the food out of the bag. She walked over to the cabinet and grabbed two plates.

"Don't play stupid with me, Marsha. You know damn well what I'm talking about. All three of us?"

Marsha put down the plates and faced Jason.

"Oh, that. I'm pregnant. I was going to wait to tell you, but..."

"The fuck you are!"

"How many times did you think you could get away with fucking me raw before this happened?"

"Because I thought you were on the pill!"

"I haven't been on the pill in months."

"No, we're not having a baby. You're getting an abortion."

"You're being silly. Why would I do that?"

"This baby is not gonna happen so get it out of your head! I will never bring a baby into this world with you."

Jason walked out of the room.

"With me? So if this baby was with Stephanie then it wouldn't be a problem, huh."

Jason walked back in and handed her some money.

"What's this for?"

"It's for your abortion. This should be enough to take care of it. Now get out!"

Jason grabbed Marsha's things and guided her towards the door.

159

"Jason, don't do this! I promise we can be a great family."

"Marsha, the next time I see you, it needs to be done."

Jason put Marsha out and slammed the door.

Stephanie awakened on the couch. Sophia walked in with a cup of coffee and stood by the couch.

"Thanks for letting me crash here last night, sis. I just couldn't go home," Stephanie said.

"It's ok. Anytime. You didn't look so well anyway."

"Gee, thanks!" Stephanie said as she smiled.

"Well, it's true."

"Is that coffee for me? I could use a cup."

"Yep, here you go," Sophia said as she handed the cup to Stephanie.

Stephanie took a sip of the coffee and quickly set it down. She jumped up and ran to the bathroom. Sophia heard her and rushed inside.

Sophia saw Stephanie on the floor with her face in the toilet.

"Oh my gosh, are you ok?"

Stephanie flushed the toilet.

"I'm on the floor with my face in a toilet. What do you think?"

"Here. Let me help you."

Sophia sat on the floor next to Stephanie. She pulled Stephanie's hair back.

"Thank you."

"You know when I first got pregnant. I was so sick. Even the smell of coffee would send me running. Oh my gosh, Steph, are you?"

"Am I what?"

"Are you pregnant?"

Stephanie raised her head.

"Noooo! I can't get pregnant. You know that," Stephanie sighed. "But that Raggedy Ann Marsha sure can."

"Well, you should take a test just in case. I still have a few boxes from when Nick and I were trying."

Sophia got up and pulled a pregnancy test out of the medicine cabinet. She extended it to Stephanie, who didn't take it.

"I don't need it. I should get my period next week, and if I don't, I guess I'll be back to get the test."

"Did you and Jason ever have unprotected sex?"

Stephanie sighed, Yes, because I didn't think I could get pregnant.

"Ok, it will be here when you need it."

Marcus sat across the street from the address that Desmond had sent him. He watched the house closely when a car that looked like Candice's car pulled into the driveway. Marcus hunched down, he didn't want to be seen. When he saw Rodney get out of the car, he snapped a picture right before he entered the house.

Marcus quickly dialed Desmond's number.

"Hey, I am outside of Trina's home and Rodney just pulled up in a car that looks like Candice's car, but I didn't see anyone else."

"Well, maybe she let him borrow her car."

"I'm going to sit here a little longer to see if I can see anyone else."

"Alright, and be careful. You might want to talk to some of the neighbors."

"Yeah, if nothing else, I can do that."

Marcus started the engine and was about to pull off when a young brown-skinned woman peeked out the door and

161

pulled the mail out of the mailbox. Marcus snapped a picture of her.

CHAPTER 20

Jason sat on the couch as he scrolled through pictures of Stephanie on his phone.

"Damn, I messed this up," Jason whispered.

Jason's phone rang, he looked in disgust as he saw the name on the screen. He swiped right.

"Hello, hello!" Marsha said.

"Did you take care of that?"

"Jason, I need to see you."

"We ain't got nothing to talk about."

"Yes, we do! Look, I'm sitting outside your place. I'm coming inside."

Jason walked over to the window and looked through the blinds. He saw Marsha walking up the walkway.

"Can we please talk, Jason?"

Jason walked over to the door and opened it.

"Look, If you ain't come to tell me you had the abortion, then we ain't got nothing to talk about."

"Jason, why are you being like this. Don't you think you're being unreasonable?'

"Hell no! You know I don't want kids," Jason said with much anger in his voice.

"No! You don't want kids with me. If I was that bitch Stephanie..."

Jason cut her off.

"Don't bring her into this. You're the one who's pregnant."

"Yeah, and if my math is correct, it takes two people to make a baby."

"Look, I'm not having this conversation."

"For your information, I have an appointment next week

at the clinic, and after it's done, you will never hear from me again!"

Marsha slammed the door as she walked out.

Later that evening, Stephanie zipped up her dress. She put on her accessories and shoes. She stared at herself in the full-length mirror. Sophia walked up behind her and put her chin on Stephanie's shoulder.

"You look amazing, sis."

Stephanie made a face. Sophia gave her a reassuring hug.

"You think so? Or are you just trying to rush me out of here?"

Stephanie went and slumped on her bed.

"Both." Sophia teased.

Sophia admired her reflection.

"I don't even feel like going anymore. Michael is still on the loose, and Karen and Susan barely got a slap on the wrist after nearly framing me."

Sophia turned to Stephanie.

"Oh no, you don't. You're not backing out of this, Steph. Do you know how much I paid for these tickets? And besides, you can't let them stop you from living!"

"I know. I'm sorry, Sophia, but..."

"But nothing! Now pull yourself together, and let's go before we're late for the comedy show.

"Ok, I'm coming."

Sophia left the room. Stephanie took one last look, sighed, then grabbed her purse and left.

Stephanie and Sophia sat in the audience. The audience roared with laughter.

"You've been a great audience! Thank you, Indianapolis!"

The audience gave a standing ovation. Stephanie turned to Sophia.

"That was so amazing! Thank you for making me come out, Soph. That was just what I needed."

"I told you, you'd like it."

Stephanie looked for the closest exit. She surveyed the area when a couple caught her eye. The woman looked so familiar. The man and woman kissed as they waited to exit their row. He playfully grabbed her booty, and then they held hands as they walked toward the exit. The woman turned her head slightly in Stephanie's direction.

"Candice?"

Stephanie squinted.

"What?" Sophia asked.

Stephanie tried to explain, but it was too loud. Stephanie rushed off to follow Candice. Sophia tried to keep up but got lost in the crowd.

Stephanie made it to the lobby. She visually searched the room for Candice and her mystery man.

"Where is she?"

Sophia walked up.

"Where is who?"

"Candice."

"Candice? Candice who?" Sophia asked.

"Desmond's Candice."

"What? Why are you looking for her?"

"Because I saw her here with another man. You know what? Nevermind. It's none of my business. Let's just go."

"Right. Why in the world would you care who she's with?"

Stephanie and Sophia left the building. They walked to the parking garage.

"I just don't understand how she can do this to Desmond. Maybe I should tell him."

"Are you kidding me? He's getting exactly what he

deserves after the way he treated you. Let him get his little feelings hurt."

"I know, but I'd never wish this on him."

"Sis, I don't care to hear any more about Desmond, okay," Sophia said as they reached her car and got in.

Rodney sat up on his side of the car and wiped his mouth. Candice sat up straight and adjusted her seat.

"Baby, that treat was so unexpected right here in the car," Candice said.

"You deserved it, and you know how I do. That's just for starters."

Rodney got out of the car, opened Candice's door, and they headed inside his place. Candice's phone rang. She looked at it and saw it was Desmond.

"It's Desmond. I might call him back."

"Answer it and be cool. We still need him."

"Hey Des, I'm at Trina's."

"Will you be home soon?"

Rodney ran his hand between Candice's legs, then kissed her on the lips.

"No, she's not feeling well, so I'm going to hang around until she falls asleep."

"Really. Can't Rodney sit with her?"

"No, she asked me."

"Ok, I have something for you when you get here."

"Ok, bye."

The next day, Marcus pulled up and sat a few doors down. He was sure about that being Candice's car.

The door opened, and there stood Candice in the doorway. She walked to her car, and Rodney stepped in the doorway and watched. Marcus took pictures. Candice drove off. A car pulled up, and the young brown-skinned woman that he saw the other day got out. Marcus took more pictures. The woman went into the home.

Marsha sat nervously waiting for the nurse to call her back to the examination room. Tears began to form as she looked around the room.

"Marsha Sanders," The nurse called out.
Marsha got up and slowly followed behind the nurse down the hallway.

"We're going to stop right here. I need to get your weight, and then we will go into room 3."
Marsha got undressed and sat on the table in a white gown as she waited for the doctor to enter. A few minutes later, there was a knock at the door.

"The doctor finished the ultrasound and looked up at Marsha."

"You're about 8 weeks pregnant. Now, are you sure this is what you want to do?"

"No! I'm ot sure at all."
Later that evening, Marsha sat on the couch alone in tears when she heard a knock at the door.
Marsha walked over and opened the front door.

"Is it done?" Jason asked as he stood at the front door.

Marcus put the flash drive in and sat back and watched the scenes from the Strip club when he came to Rodney and a female. Rodney and the female were arguing. Marcus hit pause and enlarged it when he saw Rodney and Candice.

Rodney and Candice sat at the table, making plans.

"I'll give you the key, and I won't set the alarm."

"This is going to be a piece of cake," Rodney said.

"I will start an argument a couple of days before. I will sleep in the guest bedroom so I won't have to witness this as it goes down."

"I can't believe you guys are going to do this man like

this, after all, he has done for you," Trina said with the remote control in hand flicking through the channels.

"Don't let this backfire on y'all asses," Trina commented.

"It won't, just as long as people do what they are supposed to do, that includes you, Trina."

"Me, I'm not a part of this."

"Yes, you are. You're going to be my alibi."
Trina's head bobbled.

"Alibi. Well, hell, I'm glad you told me. So when is this going down?"

"In a few days," Rodney said.

"By now, I would have thought you would have learned your lesson. When are you going to straighten up and fly right?" Trina asked.

"As soon as I get that money in my hands," Rodney said, rubbing his hands together.

"Don't you mean my hands?"

"What's yours is mine and what's mine is yours. Hasn't it always been like that?" Rodney asked.
Candice shook her head and rolled her eyes.

"Don't tell me you're having second thoughts."

"No, just remember whose name is on the life insurance policy as the beneficiary," Candice said.
Candice got up from the table, kissed Rodney on the forehead.

"I'll see you guys tomorrow," Candice said as she walked out.

Candice pulled into the driveway. She cut the engine and sat for a few minutes thinking before getting out. When she got out, Desmond stood in the doorway and greeted her as she made her way inside.

Desmond moved back and allowed Candice to enter. He shut the door and followed her down the hallway into their bedroom. Desmond stood in the doorway of their bedroom and watched Candice undress.

"You know, I have been trying to figure something out, but I can't so why don't you tell me!"
Candice stopped and turned to look at Desmond.

"What are you trying to figure out?" Candice said as she removed her shirt.

"Why are you at Trina's house so much now that Rodney is out. You are there more than you're here? It wasn't like that before."
Desmond walked to stand behind Candice. He pulled her hair from her neck and planted kisses.

"If I didn't know better, I would say you got something going on with Rodney."
He looked at Candice through the mirror. Candice turned to face Desmond.

"And why would I have something going on with my cousin's man?"

"You tell me. Is he really your cousins' man?"
Desmond turned and walked out of the room. Candice followed behind him into the kitchen.

"Why are you so fucking paranoid!"

"Because something doesn't seem right with you and Rodney's no good ass that's why!"

"You know what.... never mind," Candice said angrily.

Marcus and Officer Rodriquez were sitting in the dining room talking after dinner.

"Don't forget to leave the information you stopped by to give me."

"We're becoming quite a team Rodriquez. And thanks for agreeing to help me on another case. Here is the

169

information on the woman," Marcus said.

Marcus handed her a folder.

"Yes, we are, but things are different now."

"Yeah, I heard you got new software. Do you think it's going to take you longer to get back to me?"

"No, I'll get back to you soon. What I'm referring to, is things between us can be different now that I'm single."

She looked at Marcus, licked her lips, and slowly ran her hand over her breasts.

"... and I have needs," Rodriquez said.

"Excuse me?"

Marcus watched Rodriquez as she circled her nipple through her dress and moaned.

"You heard me. I have needs."

She kept her eyes on him. His eyes followed her hand as she moved it down the front of her stomach, past her waist and then rested it on her thigh. Marcus and Rodriquez stood, and she walked up to him. He kissed her and then pushed her away.

"I'm sorry, I shouldn't have done that."

"Don't be."

"You look so beautiful. I've never seen you like this before, but I gotta go before things go too far."

Marcus moved toward the door. As he reached the door, Rodriquez dress fell to the floor.

"Maarcuus," She said slowly.

Marcus still faced the door and looked down at the dress on the floor, then looked up at the ceiling with his hand on the doorknob.

No, she didn't just remove the straps of her dress and let it fall to the floor

"This is not happening," Marcus said under his breath.

Marcus turned his head and looked back at Rodriquez as he

opened the door. She stepped towards Marcus.

"You like?"

"Damn, thanks for the lovely evening, Rodriquez. I'll be back for the info on Candice when you get it."

Marcus stepped out the door and close it.

"You'll be back, and it won't be for paperwork," She yelled loudly.

Marcus remained standing on the outside of the door. He debated on whether he should go back inside or leave, but he decided to leave.

As Marcus walked to his car, he heard a notification on his phone, and he looked at it and saw a selfie of Rodriquez and a link to the song Pressure by Ari Lennox.

Rodney and Candice walked outside. Rodney took his jacket off and placed it around Candice's shoulders.

"Thank you, baby!"

"You know, I got you."

"I know, that's why I love you."

Rodney smiled. "I love you too."

Rodney leaned over and gave Candice a passionate kiss. Candice pulled away.

"Hmm. If I didn't know any better, I would say you're excited right now."

Rodney looked down at his manhood with a slight grin.

"You damn right, look at you!"

"So, where to next?"

Rodney waved over the man in the carriage.

"Well, since it's such a beautiful night, I thought we could take a ride."

Candice turned around. Rodney took Candice's hand and led her onto the carriage.

Candice smiled. "Oh my, you are just full of surprises tonight."

CHAPTER 21

Stephanie grabbed an ax and threw it as hard as she could. The ax hit the bullseye.

"Damn, Steph! Who are you picturing?"

Stephanie pranced over to her stool and sat next to her sister.

"You know who."

Sophia turned up her nose and handed Stephanie a beer. Stephanie opened the beer and took a swig.

"Jason?"

"You still hung up on light skin?"

Sophia stood up by the table.

"Well, you know the best way to get over a man."

Sophia bounced squat and stuck out her tongue. Stephanie waved her off.

"You're stupid," Stephanie said as she laughed.

Sophia stood up, adjusted her clothes, and grabbed an ax.

"I mean, I know you're dignified, but everyone deserves a hoe phase," Sophia said.

Sophia stepped up to the cage, threw, and completely missed the target. Stephanie and Sophia laughed. Sophia walked back to their table.

"Your advice is as bad as your aim, sis," Stephanie said.

Sophia laughed, "Girl, shut up. Who thought alcohol and axes was a good combo anyway?"

"Aww, Naw, don't go blaming it on the alcohol," Stephanie chuckled.

Sophia laughed, and then her face turned serious.

"But for real though, how are you feeling? I've been worried ever since you left my house the other day."

"Oh, I'm fine. That was nothing," Stephanie said as she looked away.

"Stephanie Marie! Yes, it was something. I found you looking a mess on my bathroom floor."

"I know. Don't be so dramatic! It was probably just stress or something."

"Did you ever take a test?"
Stephanie raised her voice. "No. And I'm not going to!"

"Well, you should! Just in case. You could be doing more harm to yourself or my little niece or nephew."
Sophia's eyes lit up.

"See! There you go. I knew this new Sophia wouldn't last. You're always butting in," Stephanie said angrily.

"I'm just looking out for you. Please promise you'll take the test soon."

"You know what? Fine! Whatever. I will, but don't get your hopes up."
Stephanie's eyes started to water. Stephanie stood and put her purse on her shoulder.
Stephanie was angry as she said, "This was fun, but I gotta go."
Stephanie snatched some money out of her purse and tossed it on the table. Stephanie hurried toward the exit as tears streamed down her face. She heard Sophia's voice call after her, but she didn't stop.

"Steph! Steph!" Sophia yelled.

Candice had her head resting on Rodney's shoulder as they rode in the carriage throughout downtown.

"Baby, this is the type of thing I want us to do every day."

"Me too, baby. I can't wait until we're together forever."

"Well, it won't be long cause our plan is in motion."

173

Rodney kissed Candice's forehead. Candice looked up at Rodney.

"You know, he thinks we have something going on because I'm always at Trina's."

"He won't have to wonder for too much longer, because he won't be a factor."

"That's right."

The carriage stopped at a traffic light. A car with dark tinted windows pulled up at the traffic light. Rodney leaned over and kissed Candice. The men in the car looked over and saw Rodney. The window started to go down slowly. The traffic light turned green, a horn blew, and the carriage proceeded.

Stephanie held the phone to her ear.

"You've reached the voicemail of Jason Santiago..."

"Dammit, Jason! Why won't you pick up the phone?"

Stephanie put the phone down; looked at herself in the large mirror, and shook her head. The positive pregnancy test and instructions lay on the counter; as the tears started and wouldn't stop.

"No, no, no! Fucccck! Not like this."

Stephanie slid down to the floor and crumpled into a ball.

"Not like this," She cried.

Stephanie awakened in bed; she got her phone and scrolled her contact list. She stopped on her OB-GYN contact and pressed the call button.

"Yes, I'd like to make an appointment," Stephanie said as she tried to hold back the tears.

Desmond looked out the window that overlooked tall high rises. Desmond suddenly turned around, walked to the phone, and pushed the speaker button.

"Yes Mr. Taylor," Cynthia said

"Cancel all my appointments, I'll be out the rest of the day."

"Okay, Mr. Taylor."

Desmond pressed the speaker button, grabbed his phone, and walked out.

Desmond sat at the bar; he grabbed his drink and tossed it back. He waved the Bartender over.

"Yeah, boss"

"Keep'em coming!"

"I think you had one too many, boss."

"I'll tell you when I've had too many!"

The Bartender shook his head; he turned around and grabbed the liquor, then poured a drink. Two men walked in and sat next to Desmond. One of the men looked at Desmond and back at the other man and nodded. The man looked at the Bartender.

"Let me get what he has," The man said.

"Sure, coming right up," The Bartender said.

Desmond was tipsy.

"I don't think you can afford what I'm drinking," Desmond said as he slurred his words.

Both men looked at each other.

"So, what are you trying to say, I don't have enough money to pay for my drinks?"

Desmond could hardly keep his head up. The man went into his pocket, pulled out a stack of money, and slammed it on the bar.

"I think I can afford everyone's drinks here, including yours."

"Look, I didn't mean to..."

"Yeah, but you did. My partner and I don't take lightly to being disrespected."

"Look, I don't want any trouble. I'm just here to clear my head."

"Sounds like you got a woman problem,"The second man said.

Both men laughed.

"It is."

Desmond slowly looked up and looked over at the men. He recognized them.

"Hey, do I know you guys?"

"No, you don't know us yet, and to be honest, I don't think you want to know us either."

"Yeah, you want and did something we didn't like, and we need you to fix it!" The second man said.

"I have no idea what you guys are talking about," Desmond said.

Desmond stood and tried to leave, but the men pushed him back down. The Bartender looked over.

"Do we have a problem here?" The Bartender asked.

The men turned to look at the Bartender. He stood at 6" 6, 350 pounds of muscle with a James Earl Jones voice.

"What's it to you?"

"What's it to me? This is my bar and my customers. So when you come in here, you will respect them!

"Ok, ok, we can respect that," One of the men said.

"When you sober up, give me a call," The second man said as he handed Desmond his business card.

Desmond got out of the Uber and staggered up the walked to the front door. He searched for his keys when the front door opened. Desmond looked up.

"What the fuck are you doing in my house?"

"Hey Des, how's it going? I hope you don't mind I used your washer & dryer because mine is on the fritz."

176

Desmond looked over at Candice.

"Why are you home so early?" Candice said.

Desmond stood with his mouth open as Candice and Rodney moved passed him and walked to her car.

"Ain't this a bitch!"

Desmond made his way inside. He pulled his tie off and kicked off his shoes as he walked down the hallway to the bedroom.

Desmond stumbled to the window and propped himself against a dresser. He saw Candice and Rodney in front of her car. Rodney smiled, leaned against Candice's car, and sexily bit his lip. She smiled, blushed, and giggled, as she looked around cautiously. Desmond watched on but could not hear the conversation. He started to open the window but reconsidered because he didn't want them to hear him. Desmond stood frozen in place as his wife flirted with another man before his eyes.

"Rodney, stop. Someone might see us," Candice said playfully.

"Like who? Homeboy in there. Shid, he won't bust a grape. He's so fucked up right now, he prolly won't remember none of dis."

"You think so? I'm getting tired of pretending. We need to end this soon before he figures it out."

"Just a little while longer. Come here, girl."

Rodney interlocked fingers with Candice and pulled her towards him for a long hug and a quick kiss.

"It's going to be alright. You hear me?" Rodney said as he hugged her.

Candice nodded and squeezed him tight. She inhaled deeply to savor the smell of his cologne.

"I got you. You're mine and always will be mine. Now, let's go."

177

Candice nodded in agreement. Rodney went around to the driver's side of Candice's car and got in. He reached over and opened the passenger side for Candice, but Candice stood by the open door.

"Maybe I shouldn't go. Don't you think I should check on him?"

"Naw. He's all fucked up. Come on. I'll have you back before he knows you are gone."

Candice got in and they took off.

Desmond saw everything.

"What the fuck! What the actual fuck! This muthafucker thinks he can just come and take my wife from me! Uggh!"

Desmond threw the dresser to the floor.

"Who does he think he is? And why does she think she can treat me this way!"

Desmond flipped the mattress off the bed. A lot of money flew from under it.

"That bitch!!! She's stealing my money too! She's going to pay for that."

Desmond grabbed all the money and stuffed it in a gym bag. He put the mattress back in place and hid the bag in his closet. He paced the floor.

"How could I have fallen for this? Stephanie would have never done this shit to me. Damn! I can't believe Candice played me."

He sat on the floor with his back against the bed frame and passed out.

Rodriquez sat on the sofa with Marcus. The lights were low, soft music played in the background, as the logs in the fireplace popped.

"Would you like some wine?"

"Yes, please," Marcus said.

Rodriquez picked up the wine bottle, poured the wine, and passed Marcus a glass.

"Thanks. Your place is quite cozy and relaxing. I might want to kick it here a minute after we talk."

"You're welcome to talk about it over dinner, and possibly dessert if you don't have anywhere to be."

"I got time," Marcus said.

"I bet you do," Rodriquez said under her breath.

They both sipped their wine in silence.

"I'm glad you have time."

"Yeah, I've had a long hard day, so what info do you have for me?"

"This."

Rodriquez stood up in front of Marcus. She opened her robe and exposed her naked body. Marcus sat his glass down on the coffee table, his face brushed up against Rodriquez's thigh. He rubbed his cheek on her thigh as she took her hand and rubbed his back. He grabbed her whole leg and squeezed it.

"Oooh I....," Marcus moaned.

Marcus stood and looked Rodriquez in her eyes.

"Going somewhere?" Rodriquez asked.

"Hell no."

Marcus pulled Officer Rodriquez in his arms and gave her a passionate kiss. She took Marcus by the hand, and they moved to the other side of the coffee table. They continued to kiss and touch each other as they lay down on the rug in front of the fireplace.

"I've dreamt of this moment for quite a while. Don't tease me, Marcus."

"I wouldn't do that. I've been trying to fight it for so long."

Marcus removed his shirt as Rodriquez pulled his pants down. Marcus kissed Rodriquez on her breasts.

"Tonight, I'm breaking all the rules and first I'm going to start with having my dessert before dinner," Marcus said.

"Oooh don't stop," Rodriquez said.

Marcus pulled into the driveway and saw the light in their bedroom still on.

"Damn! I was hoping she would be asleep."
Marcus walked through the bedroom door.

"Hey babe, what are you doing up?"
He walked over and kissed his wife. Mrs. Slay looked up at Marcus and saw the lipstick on his collar.

"Where have you been, Marcus?"

"I was working with Desmond on a case," Marcus said as he tried to avoid eye contact with his wife.
She looked at him sideways as she got out of bed and walked over to him.

"Was anyone else there?"

"What?"

"What my ass... you heard me. Was anyone else there?"

"No, just me and him," He said nervously.

"Then how did this lipstick get on your fucking collar?"
Mrs. Slay pulled at his collar as Marcus tried to move away.

"Babe, why are you tripping, ain't no lipstick on my collar."

"Trippin," Mrs. Slay said, "Take your damn shirt off so you can see it."

"Look, woman, you better go on somewhere."

"Don't let me find out you're fucking some bitch!"
Marcus shook his head as he removed his clothes. Mrs. Slay grabbed his shirt and put it in his face.

"This is what I'm talking about!"

"That ain't no lipstick."

Desmond walked into the kitchen and saw Candice at the table eating breakfast. Desmond walked over and stood on her side. He leaned over with both hands on the table.

"Let me tell you something. If I ever find another man in my home, I will fuck the both of you up!

Candice looked up at Desmond with a frightened look on her face.

"I'm sorry Des, it won't happen again. Why don't you sit down and let me fix you a plate," Candice said softly.

"Naw, I'll fix my own damn plate!"

Desmond sat down at the table and started eating. He stared at Candice as he ate. Candice avoided eye contact with him.

"So, how long have you and Rodney been fucking?"

"I'm not answering that because you're being foolish, right now."

"Foolish? You're right, it was foolish of me to leave the best thing that I had for a piece of trash."

Desmond threw his napkin on his plate and got up.

CHAPTER 22

Marcus parked his car a few houses down from Trina's. To his surprise, Rodney drove up and parked in the driveway.

"What's he doing out so early. And where'd he get that car?"

Marcus used binoculars to read the license plate. Rodney got out and went inside the house. Marcus pulled out his laptop and ran a search on the license plate.

"Candace Taylor?"

Candace ate her breakfast. She picked up her phone and texted Rodney. She placed her phone on the table and walked down the hall to the bedroom to find Desmond.

"Des! Des! Babe, can we talk?"

Candace looked around the room and saw no sign of Desmond. She walked in and saw Desmond sitting on a stool with his head in his hands.

"There you are. I know we need to talk, and I want to go first."

"What The fuck are we going to talk about Candice, huh? Nothing, absolutely nothing!"

"Des, I don't know what makes you think that Rodney and I are fucking, but it's not true."

"So now you want to make me think I'm crazy... and what I see is not real? Get the fuck outta here!"

"Des. I'm telling you the truth, I love you. I don't want him, even if he flirts with me, he is my cousin's man."

"Stop with the lying Candice, I saw him kiss you!"

Candice watched as Desmond got up and silently walked into the bedroom.

Desmond grabs his phone and keys off the dresser and left. Candice paced until she heard a door slam. She moved over to the window and saw Desmond as he drove off.

"Fuck! This has gotten out of control!"

Candice ran out of the room.

Stephanie walked to the receptionist's window.

"Hello," The receptionist said.

"Hello, I have an appointment with Dr. Franklin."

The receptionist typed on the keyboard.

"Yes, I have you here. I'll let the doctor know you're here."

"Thank you!" Stephanie said as she walked over and sat down in the chair. She looked at a man and woman who smiled and talked with each other. Stephanie smiled at the couple and got teary-eyed. A nurse opened the door.

"Mrs. Duffy." The man and woman stood up and walked through the door. Stephanie pulled out her phone and read a text message.

Hi, I'm sure, I'm the last person you ever expected to hear from. I just wanted to tell you how sorry I am for what I did to you. You never deserved to be treated that way. You are a good woman and I know I made a big mistake letting you go. I hope one day you can forgive me! Desmond

The nurse opened the door before Stephanie had time to digest the text message.

"Stephanie!" The nurse called out.

Stephanie put her phone away and stood.

Stephanie sat in the examination room for about ten minutes. She felt all kinds of emotions and willed herself not to cry.

There was a soft knock, then the doctor walked in.

"Well hello, good to see you again, Stephanie!"

183

"Hi, Dr. Franklin."

"You're not due for your wellness check up for another month, so what brings you in today?"

"Well, I think I might be pregnant."

The doctor smiled, "Congratulations! Who's the lucky man?"

"No one important."

"Does this person know you could be carrying his child?"

"No, he doesn't know and that's the way I'm going to keep it."

"What if there are important health issues that arise, doesn't he have the right to know?"

"I'll cross that bridge when I come to it. But until then, I will raise this child by myself."

"Okay, well, let's get some tests done to make it official."

Candice grabbed her phone off the table and called Rodney.

"Yeah."

"Rodney, baby, I messed up!"

Rodney sat at the table with a fresh bowl of cereal.

"Whoa, slow down. What are you talkin' 'bout?"

"I got into it with Desmond. He's on to us and I think he's coming for you."

Rodney laughed, "Coming fo' me? Naw, Johnny Cochran ain't that stupid."

Candice was frantic.

"I'm serious, Rodney! I've never seen him like this."

Rodney walked over to the window and peeped through the blinds.

"It's all good, Candy. Besides, he's got his boy watchin' the house like he's Magnum PI or somethin'."

184

"What? Oh no, this is going all wrong."

"It's coo'. Actually, it's perfect. I have no problem takin' that fool out sooner than we planned."

"Rodney, we have to do this the right way or you will end up right back in prison."

"I told you I got this."

"Yeah, that's what you said the last time."

Rodney went back to the table and enjoyed a heaping spoonful of cereal.

"Rodney, promise me we will stick to the plan."

"I can't do that. I'll try, but if he shows up here, that muthafucka might get all the smoke."

Marcus snored and awakened himself up. He looked up and saw Desmond on Trina's lawn and Rodney in the doorway. Rodney reached behind his back and wrapped his hand around his gun handle, but doesn't pull it out. Marcus rolled down his window to hear.

"Is that supposed to scare me?"

"Man, get yo punk ass out my yard befo' I give yo' wife something else to drive."

Marcus watched Desmond get in his car and leave. Rodney laughed and closed the door. Marcus called Rodriguez.

"Well, good morning."

"I need your help. How soon can we meet?" Marcus asked.

After her doctor's appointment, Stephanie went home and sat and read Desmond's message again. She called Sophia.

"Hey, this is a nice surprise."

"I wanted to tell you a secret, are you alone?"

"Yes, what is it? Why am I whispering?"

They both laughed.

Stephanie's voice cracked while talking, "Cross your fingers and pray you may be an auntie soon. I'm pregnant."

"Oh, my goodness! Congratulations Steph."

"Thank you."

"So, I was right!"

"Yes, you were, and I can't believe it! I also can't believe Desmond sent me an apology text."

"What! You have to be on a mind trip right now. Don't stress. I can't believe him."

"I know. I wanted that so bad from him and now.... well, it's good to know he has a conscience, I guess."

"Are you going to talk to him?"

"Yes."

"How did Jason react?"

"I haven't told him, I just went to the doctor to confirm everything. I'm still in a daze."

"I bet. You finally get that apology you so deserve, that has to make you feel good."

"Even though what Desmond did to me hurt, his apology made me feel like I could finally exhale."

Rodriguez and Marcus exhaled loudly as their naked bodies collided under the sheets. Rodriguez rolled off of Marcus and they lay side by side to catch their breath.

"You know, when I said I needed your help, I was referring to my case."

"Yeah, but who says we can't mix work with a little pleasure. You're lucky I had time today."

Marcus got out of bed and picked up his pants. Rodriguez took a large envelope out of the nightstand and handed it to Marcus.

"What's this?"

"Open it."

Rodriguez put on a robe and went out on the balcony. She lit a cigarette and took a puff. Marcus opened the envelope and lay the huge file on the bed.

"I looked into your mystery girl. Turns out she's got a record."

"What? How did I miss that? I ran her maiden name through all the databases."
Marcus glanced at the file while buttoning his shirt. Rodriguez put out her cigarette and came inside.

"I did too, but then I noticed that the name Candice Spencer didn't exist before 2020. Her real name is Sabrina Johnson and she has several priors."

"Oh shit! This changes everything."

"I thought it might," Rodriquez said.
Rodriguez put her arms around Marcus's neck. They kissed passionately.

"You betta stop before you mess around and get round two," Marcus said.
Rodriquez flirted, "Are you threatening an officer?"
Marcus laughed, "Yep, with a deadly weapon."
Marcus put his hand in his pants.

"Oh yeah?" Rodriquez said smiling.
Marcus dipped her onto the bed.

Marsha and Stephanie were both in the store and bump into each other.

"Wow, looky here, I'm surprised to see you in this store."

"Oh really? Don't start with me today!"

"I just figured a person in your condition or should I say your mental state would step foot in a baby store."

"And what exactly is that supposed to mean?"

"How do you do it?"

"Do what? I don't know why I'm entertaining your nonsense."

Stephanie started to walk off.

"I don't think I could shop in a baby store. I would probably order online or just give a gift card."

Stephanie turned around and replied to Marsha.

"Well, bitch, that's the difference between you and me."

"It has to bother you going to someone's else baby shower."

Stephanie smiled. "Mind your business and don't worry about me, because it will kill you to know what's going on with me!"

Stephanie noticed a woman and her little boy on the aisle and tried to talk calmly.

"Now what's hard is not whoopin yo lil ashtray up and down these aisles."

Marsha leaned in close to Stephanie and through gritted teeth, she said, "Try it I dare you."

Desmond pulled out the hospital bill from his briefcase and looked at it with a puzzled look on his face. He dialed a number on the bill.

"Hello, Indianapolis ProHealth how may I help you?"

"I'm calling about an out-of-the-country E.R. bill I don't understand."

Desmond gave the rep the info requested.

"Ok, Mr. Taylor what part of the bill are you questioning?"

"The part that states please use the E.R. for true emergencies, then my wife was charged for a physical?"

"I'll make a note in the system, but what service did your wife receive?"

Desmond lowered his voice, "She had a miscarriage."

"I'm sorry to hear that Mr. Taylor."

"Thank you. I was charged quite a bit and you guys paid your portion without questioning this?"

"The doctor notes must have made sense to our billing department for that to go through."

"Can I see the notes, or speak to the doctor?"

"Sure, you can try the contact number on the bill."

Jason lay on the couch and watched T.V. His phone buzzed, he picked it up and quickly set it back down.

"I don't know why she keep calling me, I'm done with her ass."

He looked at his phone again, picked it up, and scrolled through some picks of him and Steph.

"Damn! How did I mess this up. You are the one for me, I know that now."

Jason's phone buzzed again, Marsha's name appeared across the screen, Jason swiped right.

"How many times do, I need to tell you to stop calling me! I'm done with you!"

"And why is that, huh? Is it because you still love her, Jason?"

"Is that what you want to hear? Will it make you stop calling me? Yes, I'm in love with Stephanie. Happy?"

Marsha got emotional. "Jason with everything we've shared, how can you say this to me?"

"All, we shared was sex, that's all."

"So, I never meant anything to you?"

"You knew what it was from the beginning."

"Yeah, but, I thought maybe..."

"You thought what? That, I would fall in love with you and we would live happily ever after? My heart belongs to one woman and you ruined my chance to ever get her back."

"I can't believe you."

"Look, stop calling me! As of this moment you are blocked!"
Jason tossed the phone onto the table in frustration.

Desmond called the doctor's contact number. He finally got the doctor on the line.

"Hello Mr. Taylor, what can I do for you?" Dr. Tumacder asked.

"My wife was seen in the E.R. about 3 weeks ago by you, and I have questions about the services you billed."

"Ok and I see she did sign a release to you so what's your question?"

"I don't understand why the bill states she had a physical and doesn't state the E.R. visit was for a miscarriage?"

"Mrs. Taylor said she wanted to be the one to explain her... um situation, for the lack of a better word."

"Her situation, what do you mean?"

"Your wife was never pregnant."

"She showed me a positive pregnancy test!"

"It was probably a false read or it wasn't her test.

"Why was my wife not told this?"

"Mr. Taylor, I assure you I did, but she insisted on telling you, and to be honest, it rubbed me the wrong way."

"Really, how so."

"Your wife insisted she had a miscarriage, but it was just her menstrual cycle."

"Wow."

"I know when someone has had a miscarriage and I don't buy her story. Sorry, that wasn't professional."

"I didn't take it that way, please finish."

"Her description of what happened didn't describe a miscarriage, it's as if she faked being pregnant."
Desmond scoffs, "Oh really."

190

"She never mentioned things that a woman does that just had a miscarriage.

"She wasn't acting like one shortly after, as I think about it."

"It sounds like you have your own doubts, and at least my instincts were right."

"Thank you and can I have your office fax me those care visit notes?"

"Sure, I'll transfer you to my medical assistant."

Marcus packed an overnight bag. Mrs. Slay lay in bed with a book.

"I wish I didn't have to go, but this stakeout is going to be an all-nighter. I'll see you in the morning."

Mrs. Slay turned the page in her book. She avoided eye contact.

"Are you serious? The silent treatment? Ok, if that's how you want it."

Marcus zipped his bag and walked out of the room. Mrs. Slay threw off her robe, revealing her fully clothed body. She heard the garage door close as she left the room.

Alex opened the door with a glass of wine in her hand. Marcus stood on the other side with his overnight bag.

Ms. Rodriguez. I'm going to need you to answer some more questions," Marcus said.

"I knew you couldn't stay away."

They embraced and Alex closed the door behind him.

Mrs. Slay turned onto the street and checked her Find my Iphone app for Marcus's location. She pulled right up and recognized her husband's car.

"Stakeout my ass!"

She cut off the engine and waited about ten minutes.

"I can't do this anymore."

Mrs. Slay got out of the car and went up to the apartment.

She rang the doorbell and heard a woman's voice.

"That must be the pizza we ordered!" Alex said.

The couple opened the door widely with smiles just as wide. Mrs. Slay got an undeniable view of her shirtless husband with his arms around Alex's waist. Marcus's smile immediately fades.

Alex looked confused.

"May I help you?"

"Shit!"

Marcus let go of Alex and turned away. Alex looked at him and then back at Mrs. Slay.

"Oh, you've already helped me more than enough, sweetie. You see, that's my husband in there."

"Oh my, God."

Alex covered her face with her hands.

"Don't look so surprised, bitch! You knew he had a wife. You've known about me for years, so save it! No, better yet, call on God. Because someone just might need Him tonight if I don't leave right now!"

Mrs. Slay turned to go back to her car, but stopped to say one last thing. Alex still had the door open.

"And Marcus darling, don't even bother coming home. We're done!"

Mrs. Slay got in her car and drove off.

CHAPTER 23

Trina walked in on the phone. Rodney sat at the table, cleaning his gun, while smoking a blunt.

"Yeah baby, I'll see you later."

Trina swiped right and sat the phone on the table.

"You still kicking it with that bitch ass nigga I see."

"Look, don't worry about who I'm fucking."

"Oh, don't worry, If you want to let that nigga keep beating yo ass, who am I to get in the way of that."

"Are you done? Cause I'm really getting tired of yo shit," Trina said with anger in her voice."

"As long as you remember the plan, we good."

"Yeah, I remember the fucking plan, just make sure you do your part."

Rodney hit the blunt, grabbed the gun, and stood.

"You aint got to worry about that. Cause this nigga about to be a distant memory."

Trina rolled her eyes.

"Yeah, I can't believe Candice is willing to leave a man that's done nothing but treat her good from day one. I guess you guys are the perfect match, dumb and dumber."

Trina laughed as Rodney stood in front of her.

"So, what you don't think I'm not good enough for her?"

"Your words, not mine. But what I don't understand is if you truly love her the way you say you do, then why do you keep having her do dumb shit, which could land her in prison?

"What you say?"

"You heard me, I didn't stutter?"

"Damn you my blood, who side you on?"

"The right side, she's risking having a good life with a good man all for yo bitch ass."

Rodney fist landed across Trina's face. She fell to the floor, her face covered in blood. Rodney bent down.

"I don't give a fuck about that pussy ass nigga and after tonight, neither will she."

Rodney stepped over Trina. Trina struggled to grab her phone off the table.

Marcus pulled into the driveway and saw a car parked beside his wife's car. *Who's car is that, he wondered.*

Marcus walked in to find his wife in the study. He stood in the door, glancing at her. She looked up and rolled her eyes.

"Your things are already packed in the garage."

"Babe, can we talk?"

Mrs. Slay didn't look up. Marcus moved further into the room.

"There's nothing for us to talk about.

"I'm sorry, but it only happened once."

Mrs. Slay laughed, "Bullshit! You must think I am stupid. This is not the first time you've been with her, and it won't be the last.

Marcus looked confused.

"What are you talking about?"

"Why don't you ask her. Why do you think she's single now?"

Mrs. Slay moved and stood in front of Marcus

"You really don't know who you have been married too all these years, do you?"

Marcus took a step back as Mrs. Slay moved closer.

"You're not the only one that knows how to uncover shit about people. I've been doing it for years you just didn't

know about it. I knew about all of your little affairs and I
made sure their husbands knew."
Marcus stared at his wife.

"So what are you saying?"

"All those late nights you came home with her perfume
on you, really Marcus! Did you think so little of me?

"Baby, please, this is where I want to be. I love you!"

"You don't even know how to love a person, but guess
what, Johnny does."

"Who the fuck is Johnny?" Marcus thought back to the
driveway and the other car.

"Oh, my bad. You guys call him JP."

Marcus rushed toward Mrs. Slay and grabbed her by the
throat and slammed her up against the wall.

Johnny sat in the bedroom and heard the commotion. He
got up and rushed into the study.

Johnny saw Marcus with his hands around Mrs. Slays
throat. He grabbed Marcus and threw him onto the desk.

"Don't you ever put your hands on her again."

"Who the fuck do you think you are telling me what not
to do to **My** wife?"

Marcus ran up to Johnny.

"The man that's been keeping your side of the bed warm
at night while you're out!"

Marcus raised his fist and hit Johnny in the face. Johnny hit
the ground hard. Marcus stepped over him and walked out.

Desmond pulled into the driveway, he saw the lights on
in the living room.

Stephanie sat on the couch looking through a baby
magazine when she heard a knock at the door.

Stephanie walked to the front door with the magazine still
in her hand. When she opened the door, she was surprised
to see Desmond.

195

"Hey, Steph, how are you doing?"

"I'm good, Des. Is everything okay?"

"Not really. Can we talk?"

"Sure, come on in."

Stephanie allowed Desmond to enter. He walked into the living room as Stephanie followed behind him.

Desmond stood as Stephanie sat on the couch. He paced back and forth.

"Des, you're scaring me. What is going on?"

Desmond hesitated.

"Stephanie, I am so sorry. I've never meant to hurt you."

Desmond got down on one knee.

"You were the best thing in my life and I fucked it up for a piece of trash."

Stephanie looked surprised.

"Des, what happened with you and Candice?"

"It doesn't matter, what I want to know... is there any way you can forgive me and take me back? I've never stopped loving you."

Jason pulled up in front of Stephanie's and saw Desmond's car. He got out and walked around to the side of his car, leaned up against it with his hands in his pocket, and crossed his legs at the bottom looking at the door.

Stephanie's stood, she began to pace in front of the window.

"What the fuck! How can you come to me now and tell me this shit... why did you wait so long," Stephanie said angrily.

Stephanie shakes her head.

"Desmond... I'm pregnant," Stephanie said softly.

Desmond stood as the tears rolled down his face. He grabbed a hold of Stephanie's hands. She jerked away as her tears begin to fall.

196

"I can't do this with you right now, I just can't!" Stephanie cried.

"I'm sorry," Desmond said as he kissed Stephanie on the forehead and walked out.

Desmond walked out, and his, and Jason eyes locked. Desmond shook his head and walked to his car.

Desmond backed out of the driveway, and stopped at the end, and rolled his window down.

"Well, I guess the best man won. Congratulations, daddy."

Desmond pulled off. Jason stood with his mouth wide open.

Jason rushed up to the front door and knocked twice.

Desmond sat in the living room with a drink in his hand. He stared into space when he heard a car pull up. He figured it was Candice, he frowned, got up, and made his way to their bedroom.

Stephanie's opened the door and frowned.

"Hey, I know I am probably the last person you want to see right now."

"Yeah, pretty much."

"I know. I deserve it, I was a jerk, but I want to tell you why I was a jerk."

Stephanie stood there and looked at him, "What is this, confession night?"

Stephanie moved aside as Jason entered.

Jason followed Stephanie into the kitchen and took a seat. Stephanie fixed herself a plate.

"Are you hungry?"

"Very," Jason smiled.

"Let me guess, Marsha told you she saw me the other day and we have some not so nice words?"

"No, I haven't seen Marsha. I'm done with that."

197

"Right, I've heard that before."

"I'm serious. I am here to tell you that I am so in love with you."

Stephanie laughed, "You have got to be kidding me. Hell, I would hate to see how you would treat me if you didn't like me."

Jason got up from the table, walked over to her, and pulled her up from her seat. He raised her chin with his finger.

"Steph, I love you more than I want to and that scares me to death. I've been hurt badly and the way I feel about you..."

Jason shook his head and exhaled.

"I would be devastated if you cheated or left me for someone else. I don't like feeling the way I feel. It's scary."

"So you just decided to sabotage what we had? Jason, you're not the first person to get hurt. Getting hurt by something or someone is a part of life."

"I know that now. I thought I could get over you if I had Marsha in my life, but that only showed me how much more I loved you."

Stephanie rolled her eyes the mention of Marsha's name.

"I don't understand. You wasted all this time apart from me. You missed going to my first doctor's appoint..."

Stephanie turned her head. Jason pulled her closer to him.

"When were you going to tell me?"

"I tried to tell you. I called and texted you several times, but you never responded."

"I'm so sorry, baby. I can't imagine how you felt. Just know from this day forward, I will never leave your side."

"I don't know Jason. I never thought you would treat me the way you have. I thought you were better than that."

Candice made her way to the bedroom as Desmond dressed down to his boxers.

"You should have stayed with that nigga! I'm getting an annulment this week," Desmond said as he looked over his shoulder.

"If that's what you want to do, then do it."

Candice grabbed her night close and walked out.

Later that night, Candice sat on the side of the bed with her phone in hand. She dialed and Rodney immediately picked up.

"Is everything set up."

"Yes, I'm sleeping in the guest bedroom."

"Well, let's get this party started," Rodney sang.

At midnight at the Taylor's the home was dark and everything was quiet. Rodney quietly shut the door behind him and made his way upstairs.

Desmond was asleep when his phone buzzed. Desmond reached over and grabbed his phone. There was a text message from Marcus.

Desmond read the text message. "I just sent you an email, please check it ASAP!"

Desmond threw his legs over the bed, slipped on his house slippers, and walked to the next room to his office.

Rodney pushed open the door and saw a body in the bed. The covers were pulled over their head. Rodney looked back, turned around and pulled the trigger twice. He rushed down the stairs and out the front door.

Desmond was just about to sign onto his laptop when he heard two gunshots. He froze in place for a quick second, and then he ran into the guest bedroom.

Desmond slowly opened the guest bedroom door. He flicked the light switch on and saw Candice's body and saw the sheet covered in blood. He ran over to Candice, pulled the cover back, and saw her lifeless body.

"No! No! Candice, no!" Desmond cried out.

199

Desmond looked around and saw her phone on the night stand and called the police.

Stephanie and Jason lay asleep when her phone rang. Stephanie felt an arm wrapped around her. She glanced up at Jason and smiled. Stephanie reached over and grabbed her phone.

"What is going on?"

"Someone broke in and shot and killed Candice."

"What! Oh my God! I'll be right over!"

Stephanie hung up and shook Jason a couple of times. She told Jason what had happened.

The street and driveway were covered with police cars as Desmond's mom and father pulled up. As they walked inside, Desmond's mom eyed Stephanie and Jason and rolled her eyes. Stephanie turned her nose up as Jason chuckled.

"This is not the time nor the place. She is so fucking evil," Stephanie whispered to Jason.

The beeping of her phone awakened Rodriquez and Marcus. Rodriquez reached over and grabbed her phone.

"Are you kidding me!"

Rodriquez looked over at Marcus as she disconnected the call.

"I got to go," Rodriquez said.

"What's going on?" Marcus asked.

"There's been a murder. Go back to sleep. I'll be back shortly."

"Who's been murdered?"

Rodriquez doesn't respond. She continued to put her clothes on. Marcus got out of bed and walked over to stand in front of her.

Marcus asked sternly, "I asked who's been murdered?"

Rodriquez lifted her head.

She said softly, "Candice Taylor."
Marcus sat down on the bed.

"Oh my God! Are you serious?"
Rodriquez shook her head, "Yes."

"Do you mind if I go with you?"

"I rather you not."
Rodriquez walked inside Desmond and Candice's home. She looked around and saw Desmond in the corner speaking with her Lieutenant. She walked over and whispered into his ear.

"Can I speak with you outside?" Rodriquez asked.
Lieutenant Sampson and Rodriquez stood outside talking. She explained that she has been working with Mr. Slay and what they discovered.

"So, do you think he did it?"

"Everything points to him, "Rodriquez said as she handed him a flash drive.

"Everything we found is on this. I say we take him in until you review what we found."

Lieutenant Sampson walked over to Desmond, who was talking to his Parents.

"Desmond, you have the right to remain silent. Anything you say can or will be held against you in the court of law. If you can't afford an attorney, one will be provided for you," Lieutenant Sampson said.
Desmond stood as the room spun, the voices were muffled.

"Oh the hell you will. My son wouldn't hurt anyone," Mrs. Taylor shouted.

"Ma'am, please step back or you will be arrested along with your son," Rodriquez said.

"This bitch!" Mrs. Taylor yelled.
Mr. Taylor grabbed his wife, covered her mouth with his hand, and took into the kitchen.

201

Jason and Stephanie stood and watched as Desmond was escorted out in handcuffs.

End of Part Two

BETRAYAL 2

Made in the USA
Middletown, DE
24 July 2022